Enid Blyton

THE NAUGHTIEST GIRL

Keeps a Secret

D1146991

Have you read them all?

Enid Blyton

THE NAUGHTIEST GIRL

Keeps a Secret

Illustrated by Kate Hindley

Hodder
Children's
Books

a division of Hachette Children's Books

Text copyright © Hodder & Stoughton Ltd, 1999
Illustrations copyright © Hodder & Stoughton Ltd, 2014

First published in Great Britain in 1999 by Hodder Children's Books
This edition published in 2014

The right of Enid Blyton to be identified as the Author of
the Work has been asserted by her in accordance with the
Copyright, Designs and Patents Act 1988

1

All rights reserved. Apart from any use permitted under UK copyright
law, this publication may only be reproduced, stored or transmitted, in
any form, or by any means with prior permission in writing from the
publishers or in the case of reprographic production in accordance with
the terms of licences issued by the Copyright Licensing Agency and
may not be otherwise circulated in any form of binding or cover other
than that in which it is published and without a similar condition
being imposed on the subsequent purchaser.

All characters in this publication are fictitious and any resemblance
to real persons, living or dead, is purely coincidental.

A Catalogue record for this book is available from the British Library

ISBN 978 1 444 91886 1

Printed and bound in Great Britain by
Clays Ltd, St Ives plc

The paper and board used in this paperback by Hodder Children's Books
are natural recyclable products made from wood grown in sustainable
forests. The manufacturing processes conform to the environmental
regulations of the country of origin.

Hodder Children's Books
a division of Hachette Children's Books
338 Euston Road, London NW1 3BH
An Hachette UK company

www.hodderchildrens.co.uk

CONTENTS

INTRODUCTION

by Cressida Cowell

bestselling author of the
How to Train Your Dragon series

Like so many, many children before and after me, Enid Blyton's books played a crucial role in turning my nine-year-old self into a passionate reader.

That is because Enid Blyton had an extraordinary knack for writing the kind of books that children actually *want* to read, rather than the kind of books that adults think they *should* read.

Enid Blyton could tap into children's dreams, children's desires, children's wishes, with pin-point accuracy. She knew that every child, however good and well-behaved they might look on the outside, secretly longed to be Elizabeth Allen, the naughtiest kid in the school. I'm afraid I entirely cheered Elizabeth on, as she defied her parents, the headmistresses, her schoolmates, and the very serious School Meetings. If anything, I wanted her to be even naughtier.

But the Naughtiest Girl books were really my favourite of Enid Blyton's school stories because of Whyteleafe, a very different school from Malory Towers or St Clare's. What if there could be a school in which discipline was administered by the children rather than the adults? In which all money was given in at the start of the term and distributed amongst the children along socialist lines? Wouldn't this be the kind of school that children would actually *want* to go to, rather than the kind of school that children *have* to go to?

It was an interesting proposition to a nine-year-old, and it remains an interesting proposition.

I hope you enjoy this story as much as I did when *I* was nine years old.

Cressida Cavell

CHAPTER ONE

A MESSAGE FROM WILLIAM AND RITA

'IT'S STILL lovely and sunny!' said Elizabeth happily, as she came out of the first form classroom with her friend Julian and his cousin, Patrick.

It was four o'clock in the afternoon. Lessons at Whyteleafe School had finished for the day. Along the corridor, boys and girls were bursting out of other classrooms, laughing and chattering noisily. Soon everyone would change out of school uniform, go to tea, then race off to take part in all their summer term activities.

There was always so much to do at Whyteleafe, thought Elizabeth. She loved it here now. She was still a monitor, though only an honorary one this term. There were no silly quarrels to worry about at present, no misunderstandings, no having to keep her temper. She and Patrick were just starting to get on reasonably well too. At the beginning of term they had been sworn enemies.

1

THE NAUGHTIEST GIRL KEEPS A SECRET

'This is my favourite time of year!' Elizabeth told Julian. 'The evenings are so light and long. It gives you time to fit everything in. I think I'll do some gardening later. I'm sure my lettuces need watering . . .'

'You've got to come and watch my tennis match first,' Patrick butted in.

Elizabeth nodded that she would, then continued.

'To think how much I hated it here at the beginning. It seems so strange now. I did everything I could to try and get myself sent home.'

'You mean, last summer, when you were the naughtiest girl in the school?' asked Julian, his green eyes showing his amusement. 'Wish I'd been here then. Poor Elizabeth. You've been trying to live it down ever since.'

'Well, I *have* lived it down,' said Elizabeth firmly.

'She wouldn't be a monitor if she hadn't,' Patrick pointed out. 'Anyway, it wasn't all that strange. Hating it here at the beginning, I mean. Look at me: three weeks ago I couldn't stand the place!'

It was true. Julian's cousin was new this term. And, although the two cousins looked rather alike, their characters were very different. Julian was lively and jokey, full of a self-confidence which came from being so clever and good at everything. He didn't, for example, in the least mind Elizabeth being a monitor. Patrick, when he'd first arrived, had been sullen and lacking in confidence. And he had deeply resented a girl telling him what to do.

'But you do like it here now, don't you, Patrick?' said Elizabeth.

'Not so terrible having a school with girls in it, is it?' said Julian, wryly. 'And you've got your trial for the second tennis team. Already! I call that good going.'

'Yes, not bad.' Patrick flushed with pride. 'Don't you two forget to come and watch me, either. I need supporters.'

'We'll come and support you,' piped up a voice in the corridor, just behind them. It was Arabella Buckley, with a friend. 'We'll come and cheer Patrick on, won't we, Rosemary?'

'Of course we'll come!' said Rosemary, who always agreed with everything Arabella said.

'We'll be there, Patrick,' said Elizabeth quietly. 'You know you can do it. I'm sure you can beat Roger.'

Roger Brown was a big boy, in his last term at Whyteleafe. But even so, he was only clinging on to his place in the school's second team by his fingertips.

Mr Warlow, the sports master, had watched Patrick play. He had also noted how hard the new boy practised each day. So a trial had been arranged.

After tea today, Roger and Patrick were to play

singles against each other. Everybody knew that if Patrick proved to be the stronger player, he would be awarded that precious place in the second team.

'You'll need that special racket of yours though, Patrick,' said Julian. 'Better not let Elizabeth get anywhere near it. You know what she's like.'

He kept a straight face as he said it. For a moment Elizabeth took him seriously.

'Julian Holland, what a hateful thing to say—'

Once, in a fit of rage with Patrick, Elizabeth had caused his lovely new racket to get soaked with rain. She hated to be reminded of it now.

It was Patrick who quickly smoothed things over. 'Don't worry! I'll guard it with my life!' he smiled.

Elizabeth smiled then, too, and the awkward moment passed.

At teatime, she even managed to make a joke at her own expense.

Patrick had changed into his tennis things and come over to join Elizabeth's table, carrying his precious tennis racket. It really was his pride and joy.

'If anything can bring me luck, it's this,' he told John McTavish. 'I'm useless with any other racket.'

'Better not leave it by my chair then, Patrick,' said Elizabeth. 'I think you ought to padlock it to the table leg. You know what I'm like!'

A MESSAGE FROM WILLIAM AND RITA

All the boys and girls at the table laughed. Julian gave Elizabeth's arm an approving pinch. He was pleased to see his friend not taking herself too seriously.

Arabella, however, turned her pretty little doll-like face towards Patrick and smiled primly.

'It wasn't so funny at the time, though, was it, Patrick?' she said.

Elizabeth ground her teeth.

She tried hard to think of something clever to say, to get back at Arabella. But at that moment, someone came hurrying over to their table.

'Elizabeth?'

'Joan!'

Elizabeth was always pleased to see her special friend. But Joan was older and had gone up to the second form quite quickly, so the two girls saw less of each other these days. Elizabeth knew that if she did well at lessons this term she, too, would go up in September. Then she and Joan would be together again. Elizabeth was looking forward to that.

'I've got a message for you,' said Joan softly. She was always quietly spoken. 'It's from William and Rita. They would like you to come along to their study after tea, please.'

Elizabeth frowned in surprise. William and Rita were the head boy and the head girl of Whyteleafe School.

'Are you coming too? Are all the monitors coming?' Elizabeth asked. She was puzzled because there was no school Meeting due for a day or two yet.

Sometimes all the monitors were called in if there was something important to discuss before the Meeting. The Meeting was held once a week. All pupils had to attend. It was a kind of Parliament. At Whyteleafe it was the boys and girls themselves who made many of the important rules and saw that they were applied fairly. When problems arose, they sorted them out themselves. The teachers rarely had to be involved.

'No, they just want you,' said Joan. 'I don't know what it's about.'

Elizabeth rushed through her tea after that. What did William and Rita want to see her about?

'Hey, Monitor, don't gobble your food. You're supposed to set a good example,' teased Julian. 'William and Rita aren't going to disappear down a big hole. They can wait,' he added, carelessly.

'I'll finish up your scrambled egg if you can't manage it all, Elizabeth,' said her friend Kathleen, all smiles and rosy cheeks as usual.

'Would you really like it?' asked Elizabeth, gratefully. 'Cook's given me too much. Then I can slip off and see what they want with me. I haven't done anything bad lately, have I, Kathleen?'

She picked up her remaining chocolate biscuits, put them in her pocket, scraped her chair back, then got up and left the table.

'If you'd done anything bad it would have to wait for the Meeting, Elizabeth!' Julian called after her, 'and the whole school would have to hear about it. You know that's the system here. See you later!'

'Come straight on to the tennis-courts!' Patrick added. 'I'll be playing soon.'

But Elizabeth, hurrying out of the hall, didn't hear them. The chatter and clatter from other tables filled her ears and drowned out the boys' voices.

There was only one thought in her mind at present.

Why had the head boy and girl asked her to come and see them?

CHAPTER TWO

ELIZABETH UPSETS PATRICK

'COME IN,' called the head boy, as Elizabeth tip-tapped nervously on the study door.

It was a lovely, sunny room with a big window. William and Rita were sitting in their armchairs.

Rita pointed to the visitor's armchair. 'Do sit down, Elizabeth.' She was smiling and speaking kindly.

William was smiling, too.

The little girl's heart stopped beating quite so fast. She sat down in the visitor's armchair with its cheerful chintz cover.

'We've got a problem,' explained William. 'We have discussed it with Miss Belle. But now we'd like your advice. We would like to know what you think.'

Miss Belle! Elizabeth's chest swelled with pride. Miss Belle and Miss Best were the joint headmistresses of Whyteleafe School. The children called them The Beauty and The Beast. If Miss Belle were involved in this, then it must be an important matter on which her opinion was being sought.

ELIZABETH UPSETS PATRICK

Rita decided they should get it over quickly.

'The fact is, we shouldn't really have thirteen monitors,' she said. 'It's always been the tradition that we have twelve. And as I'm sure you've noticed at the Meetings this term, Elizabeth, it's almost impossible to get thirteen chairs on the platform. There's always one person practically falling off the end.'

Elizabeth nodded. She *had* noticed that.

It had all come about because, owing to lots of misunderstandings last term, Elizabeth had lost her position as monitor. A second former, Susan, had been elected in her place. But then, at the end of term, when all the misunderstandings had been sorted out, the first form had asked for Elizabeth to be reinstated, as an honorary monitor.

'For once, in a way, we must have an extra one', Miss Belle had agreed. For she knew how much Elizabeth wanted to prove herself a good, wise and sensible monitor, after some of the reckless things she had done.

'It seemed such a lovely idea to have an extra monitor at the time,' continued Rita. 'But we've discussed it with Miss Belle and we're all agreed that it can't be a permanent arrangement.'

William looked straight at Elizabeth.

'We've been wondering whether we should ask Susan to stand down, Elizabeth. What do you think?'

'Poor Susan! That wouldn't be fair!' exclaimed Elizabeth without hesitation. 'She has had hardly any time as a monitor! And she *was* elected by the whole school, with proper votes and everything . . .'

Her voice tailed away. She swallowed very hard. There was no alternative.

'Let *me* stand down,' she said nobly, with a weak, wobbly smile. 'I've had a good turn as a monitor now. I wanted to prove myself—'

'You have certainly done that, Elizabeth,' said Rita.

'Good kid,' said William softly. 'Are you quite sure, Elizabeth? We could ask Susan, you know. She was only elected because of the misunderstandings about your behaviour.'

'I am quite sure,' said Elizabeth, somehow managing to keep that brave, wobbly smile in place. She wanted to rush away now, as fast as she possibly could.

'Well done, Elizabeth,' said Rita. 'William will announce it at this week's Meeting then.'

As Elizabeth left the study, William held open the door for her. He gave her a pat on the back as she went.

'You will be elected monitor again one day, Elizabeth. I am quite sure of that.'

'Thank you, William,' replied Elizabeth, feeling very noble.

She was proud of herself for being so calm and

sensible in front of William and Rita, but as soon as the study door closed behind her, she felt a hot prickling sensation behind her eyes. She was going to cry! She must run somewhere safe, where nobody could see her.

No longer a monitor!

She needed to be alone. She needed time to think, to get over the shock. Where could she go? Where was quiet and unhurried – peaceful?

The school gardens. She often went there when she wanted to think.

She made a beeline for the gardens at once. She shut herself in the farthest greenhouse.

Then she let the tears flow.

'It's not fair!' she sobbed. 'It's not, not fair!'

She forgot all about Patrick and his tennis trial. She forgot that she had promised to come and support him.

Patrick's hopes and dreams had completely slipped her mind.

'Pull yourself together, Elizabeth Allen,' she told herself, some time later. 'Stop being a silly baby. It's perfectly fair and you know it is.'

She dried her eyes as best she could. She put her sodden handkerchief away in her pocket. Then she peeped cautiously through the greenhouse windows.

There were very few people around. There was no

sign of John Terry, the senior boy who ran the school gardens. Good. She did not feel like facing anyone yet, not even John. He was the most kind and understanding of boys, of course. He cared nothing for important positions, monitorships and the like, only for his beloved garden. John was a genius at growing things and at teaching others how to grow them. With his team of volunteers, he helped to provide enough fresh fruit and vegetables to supply the kitchens at Whyteleafe School for much of the year.

Even so, she wanted a little more time on her own.

'Elizabeth,' she told herself, 'you will no longer be a monitor after this week's Meeting. Just get that into your head! It's perfectly fair. And you've got to accept it!'

She felt rather cross with herself for not having foreseen this. It was quite true that since the beginning of term it had been uncomfortable and awkward having an extra chair on the platform at Meetings. She should have offered to stand down earlier! But it was such fun being a monitor, you wanted it to go on forever. So she had simply buried her head in the sand, as an ostrich does when it sees trouble ahead.

'All good things come to an end, Elizabeth,' her last governess used to tell her. 'And sometimes sooner than you expect.'

ELIZABETH UPSETS PATRICK

Elizabeth had never listened to a word that Miss Scott said. She blushed to think how rude she had been. Of all the awful things she had said, not only to Miss Scott but to the long line of governesses before her. Not surprisingly, none of them had ever stayed very long. But now she realized Miss Scott had been speaking sense, after all.

'But Rita says I've proved I can be a good monitor. And William says my turn will come again.'

Elizabeth began to feel more cheerful. It was very warm in the greenhouse. She went and opened the door wide and stood there for a while, gazing out.

The sun was sinking lower. A gentle breeze was making rustling sounds in the blackcurrant bushes. Somewhere a blackbird was singing. A sweet, warm scent wafted from the wallflowers that bordered the nearest vegetable plot. There were butterflies settled there, sharing the flowers with the buzzing bees. In a reverie, Elizabeth found her chocolate biscuits, rather warm and sticky by now. She ate them slowly, a melting mouthful at a time.

'There's more to life than being a monitor,' Elizabeth decided. 'I shall have more time to myself. I must try and get good at lots of things. I shall make myself learn to be a brilliant gardener and grow wonderful things.'

She stared at the neat rows of broad beans that John

and some of the younger boys had planted. How well they seemed to be doing. Although they did need weeding.

Most of Elizabeth's efforts to grow things so far had come to grief, usually because she had forgotten to look after them properly. But she knew that her lettuces were doing well. She closed the greenhouse door behind her and slowly walked round to have a look at them.

'They've grown again!' she exclaimed as she came round the corner.

She had spent some of her own allowance on lettuce seeds. John had told her it was always worth getting the very best quality. She had planted the seeds out in neat rows, watched them grow into tiny lettuces, weeded them carefully once a week. Now she was beginning to get her reward.

The lettuces had suddenly burgeoned. Some of them had formed proper hearts. They were beginning to look like real lettuces. At this rate, they would be ready before half-term. *Her* lettuces would be going into lots of school salads. That thought made Elizabeth feel very proud.

'But they *do* need watering, poor things,' she realized. 'The ground all round them is quite parched looking. I'll go and fill the watering cans.'

The two watering cans were lined up by the garden

tap. Before filling them, Elizabeth turned on the tap and cupped some water in her hands. She washed the chocolate off her hands then doused her face clean. Now nobody would be able to see that she had been crying.

She filled the watering cans but, when she reached her lettuce rows, she stopped. Was there still some heat in the sun? John had once explained to her that watering should be done in the cool of the day, morning or evening.

So Elizabeth set to work weeding between the rows of broad beans, instead. It was hard physical work and it had a wonderfully soothing effect on her. By the time she had finished she felt glowing with good health, and much more at peace with herself. She could face the world now.

'I'm getting quite used to the idea of not being a monitor,' she told herself. 'I shan't tell anyone yet. I'll wait till it's announced at the Meeting. That will give me a bit more time to get really calm and strong about it. I expect Julian will tease me. I hope Arabella doesn't crow.'

The sun was now much cooler. Elizabeth returned to her lettuces and carefully watered each row. She had just finished when John Terry appeared.

There were other boys and girls arriving, too. She could hear their voices beyond the yew hedge.

'That's well done, Elizabeth. Just the right amount of water,' he said. 'You don't want to drown them. They're doing well, aren't they?'

'Do you think so, John?'

'I'll tell you something, though. This is the last time you'll have to water them for a while.' He looked up at the sky. 'This is the end of the sunshine. There's going to be heavy rain for two or three days.'

Like any good gardener, John always took careful notes of the weather forecast.

'Oh. Is there? But it will save me a job, then!' said Elizabeth cheerfully.

'Well, it will save you one job. But it could give you another. You see, Elizabeth—'

'John!' someone shouted.

Before John could finish, a boy came marching over, carrying a garden fork.

'Where exactly do you want this ground turned over?' asked the boy.

'I'll show you in a minute. I just want to explain something to Elizabeth.'

But Elizabeth was staring at the new arrival in dismay. He was a large, heavily-built boy, one of the oldest in the school. He often came and helped in the gardens. He had big feet and big red hands and a gentle face. Elizabeth noticed how pale he looked,

16

as though he were unwell. He was still in his tennis shorts. It was Roger Brown, Patrick's tennis opponent.

The match must be over!

Patrick's tennis trial! It had gone right out of her mind!

'It's all right, John, I've got to dash now!'

Elizabeth started running.

'Tell me another time. I've realized I shouldn't be here!' she called back.

She ran as fast as she could, all the way to the tennis-courts.

Patrick was sitting on a bench near the courts with Julian, surrounded by first formers.

Elizabeth raced towards them, panting for breath.

'Did you win, Patrick?' she shouted.

'Of course he did!' shrilled Arabella.

'Elizabeth!' exclaimed Julian. 'What happened to you? Why didn't you come?'

Elizabeth went very red.

'I forgot,' she said.

'Patrick won!' cried Arabella triumphantly. 'He's going to be in the second team! It made all the difference to him having his friends here, cheering him on. Fancy you just forgetting to come, Elizabeth.'

Elizabeth thought how horrible it sounded, put like that.

She pushed past Arabella to get to Patrick, her hand outstretched. She wanted to shake his hand.

'Congratulations, Patrick. You really deserve to be in the team after all your hard work! I truly meant to come and watch the match. I'm sorry. It's just that, after I'd been to see William and Rita, I had such important things—'

She broke off. She had been going to say 'such important things to think about'. But that sounded bad, too, as though Patrick's tennis trial was *not* important.

In any case, Patrick was ignoring her outstretched hand. He was getting to his feet.

'I've got important things to do as well,' he said. 'Now I'm in the second team, I've got to do some more work on my service action. I'm going to have a good go against the school wall. There's a match on Saturday.'

Without even glancing at Elizabeth, he strode away. There was a sulky expression on his face. He was overjoyed to have beaten Roger and to have won his place in the team. But he had been wondering what had happened to Elizabeth. He had even, in fact, been worrying about her. Whereas she, it seemed, had simply forgotten all about him!

What were these important things, anyway?

Later, he learnt from young Peter what Elizabeth had been doing while his match was in progress. She

had been weeding some vegetable plot in the school gardens. Peter had seen her there.

That was all. Weeding! Even Julian's eyebrows shot up in surprise when Patrick passed on this information.

'She's good at heart though, Patrick,' he shrugged. 'You'll find that out.'

Elizabeth had no intention of confessing to Julian, far less to Patrick, that she had been crying like a baby in the greenhouse. But she would go out of her way to be nice to Patrick, she decided. Then he would soon forget her lapse.

In fact, by cocoa-time that evening, Patrick was already in a mood to forgive Elizabeth and give her another chance. His serving practice had gone well and he was very excited about the match against Woodville on Saturday.

'It's a home match, so you'll have to come and watch,' he told Elizabeth. 'Especially as you're a monitor.'

Elizabeth smiled wryly, thinking of the surprise in store for them all at the weekly Meeting. She chose her words with care.

'Monitor or not,' she said, 'I'll be there.'

CHAPTER THREE

PATRICK MAKES A LITTLE JOKE

IT WAS time for the weekly Meeting. The whole school was required to attend. The boys and girls looked forward to it. It was the day their money was given out. After that, there were always complaints to be heard and interesting things to discuss.

It had been raining for two days and outdoor hobbies had been cancelled, even riding. They were pleased to have the Meeting coming up after tea to liven things up. The weather was supposed to get better by the evening, much to Patrick's relief. He was longing to get more practice before Saturday's match.

All the children trooped into the gym, which doubled as the school hall. In the Easter holidays, a platform had been built at one end for the school's little plays and concerts. It made the Meetings much better, too. There was a long row of chairs up on the platform, facing into the hall. There sat the school's twelve elected monitors, six each side of the head-boy and girl.

William and Rita, in the centre, sat behind a small table. On the table was a Big Book, in which lots of things were written. By the Book lay a small hammer, which they used like a Judge's gavel. They *were* rather like Judges, with their Jury alongside them, Elizabeth always thought. This was not only the school's Parliament, where problems were discussed and rules made, it was also its Court. All complaints of bad behaviour or wrongdoing had to be brought to the Meeting. Problems were aired in public, punishments decided upon if necessary. Above all, boys and girls were made to face up honestly to their faults.

Miss Belle and Miss Best, the joint headmistresses, sat right at the back of the hall, with Mr Johns, the senior master. They rarely took any part in the proceedings and only then if their advice was requested.

Elizabeth had hated the Meetings when she first came to Whyteleafe School. She had thought them a perfectly silly idea. She had since changed her opinion.

But where was she today?

'That's funny,' said Julian, as he filed into the hall with the rest of the first form. He was staring towards the platform. 'Why isn't Elizabeth up there with the other monitors?'

'She must be late,' giggled Belinda.

'But there's no chair up there for her, either.' Julian

was always very quick to notice things. 'It's odd.'

Elizabeth had still not told anybody. It had been too early to tell, she had reasoned. It would come out at the Meeting. She would be quite composed by then. That would be soon enough.

'I wonder what's going on?' mused Julian now.

He did not have to wait long to find out.

All the benches in the hall had filled up. Some of the younger children sat cross-legged on the floor. They were in the junior class, which was below the first form. The babble of whispering and chattering was getting louder and louder.

William stood up and banged the gavel.

'Silence, please.'

There was an instant hush.

'Before the Meeting starts, I have something to say.'

He smiled down at the person who was perched on the very end of a bench, in the front row.

'Stand up, please, Elizabeth. Come up here, on to the platform.'

As she stood up, for all her resolve, Elizabeth found her legs going wobbly. She felt butterflies in her tummy. The whole school was looking at her. She had so hoped that William or Rita would just make the announcement very quickly and quietly. This was awful.

Determined to look dignified, she walked slowly up on to the platform.

Julian and the others watched in surprise. It was their very own Elizabeth. The bold, bad girl. What was all this about?

'For much of last term, Elizabeth was a monitor,' William told the school. 'This term, as a special dispensation, we asked her to stay on for a while – as an honorary monitor. We were so proud of her, weren't we? Well, she has done a really good stint and the time's come for Elizabeth to stand down now. I think we are all agreed that she has been a very fine monitor indeed. I want us all to show our appreciation.'

He gave a brief nod. Rita rose from her chair. Then all twelve monitors on the platform did likewise. As William shook Elizabeth by the hand, the head girl and monitors gave her a standing ovation.

The whole school joined in. With her head held high, Elizabeth came down from the platform. As she walked down the hall to join her own form's benches, children on all sides started cheering loudly. After two days of being cooped up indoors it was good to have an excuse to shout and cheer!

Elizabeth felt weak with relief. The experience had not been humiliating, after all. It had been just the reverse. How tactfully William and Rita had handled it.

She felt buoyed up, almost cheerful.

'You dark horse,' whispered Julian, as she sat down beside him. Belinda, Kathleen, even Patrick, they all slapped her on the back. Patrick had reason to know how good a monitor she had been but was secretly relieved. He would never get used to the idea of girls being allowed to boss boys around. This would be better, he felt.

Arabella was clapping politely, for quite the wrong reasons.

Julian squeezed Elizabeth's arm. 'Brave girl!' he hissed, green eyes twinkling. Alone amongst the first formers, he had continued to be curious to know why William and Rita had summoned her the other day. He had been mystified that Elizabeth, usually so talkative, had never referred to it. Now he understood.

Elizabeth simply gave a huge sigh of relief. William was banging his gavel and calling for silence again; time to get on with the Meeting. Thank goodness *that* was all over!

Thomas held up the big money-box now. All the children who had been sent money during the past week had to come forward and drop it inside. After that, every member of the school was handed two pounds from the box, as their spending money for the week.

THE NAUGHTIEST GIRL KEEPS A SECRET

At Whyteleafe School they did not believe in some children having more money to spend than others. This was the way they shared it out fairly. If any pupil wanted extra money for a special purpose, they had to ask. The Meeting then decided if it was a proper reason.

'Please, I left all my stamps out in the rain and now they're useless,' said Peter, standing up. 'I need to write some letters this week. Can I have some extra money to buy more stamps?'

No, the stamps getting all messy and stuck together was due to Peter's own carelessness, the Meeting decided.

'You'll just have to go without a few sweets this week,' Rita said kindly.

Mary wanted the Florist Shop in the village to send some flowers to her aunt, who was very ill in hospital.

'Request granted,' said the head-boy. 'Thomas, give Mary an extra five pounds from the box.'

After that there were three complaints to be heard. Two were proper complaints and one was silly.

'Arabella Buckley keeps making faces at me in class,' said Daniel Carter. 'She keeps trying to make me laugh. And if I do laugh, I'll get into trouble.'

'That is not a proper complaint,' said William sternly. 'That is just telling tales. Sit down at once, Daniel.'

The first form were making spluttering sounds as they tried not to giggle.

'Try looking the other way, Daniel!' whispered Belinda.

'Arabella's not making faces!' hissed Julian. 'She always looks like that!'

Arabella, who had been feeling so triumphant, turned bright pink. She prided herself on her prettiness.

William banged the table again.

'Before we close the Meeting, some congratulations are in order. Roger, stand up please.'

The big senior boy shambled to his feet. He was embarrassed to be in the limelight. His gentle face, even at the best of times, wore a slightly anxious look. It was just his normal expression.

'As we know,' said William, 'Roger is in the top class and in his last term at Whyteleafe. He has just heard recently that he has won a scholarship to Holyfield School. An academic scholarship. Well done, Roger. Can we give him a round of applause, please?'

As everyone clapped, Roger Brown gave a shy nod then quickly sat down.

'Isn't Holyfield the sporty school?' whispered a second former, to one of his classmates. 'Will he get on all right there?'

Everyone knew he'd lost his place in the second tennis team, to a mere first former.

'They have other people as well,' the friend whispered

back. 'People who are musical or just plain brainy, like Rog. He should be all right!'

The first formers, as they trooped out of the hall, were much more interested in the news about Elizabeth.

'You can be ordinary Elizabeth Allen now,' said Belinda, kindly. 'It will give you more time for riding and everything.'

'Will it feel funny, not being a monitor any more?' asked Kathleen.

'Just for a while, I expect,' replied Elizabeth calmly.

The boys teased her a bit, especially Julian.

'Now you can go straight back to being the naughtiest girl in the school again!' he laughed.

'Never!' retorted Elizabeth. She was standing up to the teasing well.

But then Patrick struck a discordant note.

'Of course, there's no need for you to come and watch me play in the school match now,' he said. 'I won't want you there if you're not an important monitor.'

He was trying to make a joke. But Patrick's jokes were always rather heavy-handed.

His words really stung. For a moment, Arabella and some of the others noted the look of dismay on Elizabeth's face.

By the time the little girl realized that he was not being serious, the main doors had been opened and everybody was whooping and rushing outside. It had stopped raining at last! It was going to be a fine evening.

'Hurray!' cried Patrick. 'I'll go and get my racket and practise my strokes.'

'I must go over to the stables and see the horses!' exclaimed Robert.

People were scattering in all directions.

'My lettuces,' thought Elizabeth. 'I can go and look at them. I'm sure the rain won't have washed them away. They weren't little babies any more. I wonder if they've grown?'

Luckily Elizabeth went and changed into her black wellies first, for there were puddles on all the paths in the school gardens. The big vegetable garden was all muddy and squelchy. She picked her way through the blackcurrant bushes, where the weak sunshine glistened on the wet leaves. Then, on past the dripping yew hedges to where her lettuces lay . . .

She gave a gasp of dismay.

'Oh, no!'

She stood and stared at her rows of lettuce, unable to believe her eyes. Only three days ago they had been such fine specimens, all plumping out nicely and forming hearts. Now they were unrecognizable.

'They're all chewed up. They look horrible—'

UGH! As she bent to touch the nearest plant, a fat

black slug slid off it. Gazing along the rows she saw another slug, then another. They were feasting on her lettuces! They must have been feasting on them for days.

'Elizabeth?'

John Terry appeared, carrying a large white jug.

'Oh, John. Look! Look! Horrible slugs. Big, fat, black ones. They've eaten all my lettuces. They've ruined them!'

He came and put an arm round her shoulders.

'I know,' he said, sadly. He looked down at her disappointed face. 'Poor Elizabeth! This was what I was trying to warn you about the other day, when they said there was rain on the way. If only you hadn't been in such a hurry—'

'You mean you *knew* this might happen?'

'When it's very wet we nearly always get an epidemic of slugs here. There are things you have to do about it.'

'But what, John? I don't understand.' Elizabeth frowned. Oh, *why* had she rushed away the other evening, just to hear about Patrick's silly tennis trial? Why hadn't she stopped and listened to John! 'What *can* you do?'

'Come with me and I'll show you.'

Still carrying the jug, he led her to a warm, sheltered part of the garden. There stood two rows of the finest looking lettuces anyone could hope for. One row consisted of the round variety, the other of the cos variety.

'The slugs have hardly got to them at all!' exclaimed Elizabeth in surprise.

'These are mine,' said John quietly. 'They're extra special, so I've had to take good care of them. We get slugs in this part of the garden, too, though not as many. But look, come along the rows with me and you'll see.'

For the first time, walking down the two rows with John, Elizabeth noticed there were old bowls placed at intervals, six of them in all. They were deep little bowls, old and chipped. Formerly school soup bowls, but long since thrown out. Elizabeth crouched down and peered inside one.

'It's full of dead slugs!' she shrieked.

'They all are,' replied John. 'They've all been drowned! Now, watch what I do, and I'll explain.'

John put down his jug. Then, working quickly, he gathered up the bowls two at a time. He tipped the bowlfuls of slimy, dead slugs on a nearby rubbish heap, then replaced the empty bowls in position.

'Some people put down pellets to kill slugs,' he told her. 'But that can be cruel. Pellets can harm other creatures, too. This way is much better.'

He asked Elizabeth to hand him the jug.

'Is there milk in here?' she asked, sniffing. 'It smells a bit off.'

'It is,' smiled John. 'Cook always has plenty of old milk left over. It doesn't matter if it's a bit sour. I cadge it off her.'

He went round his lettuces, slurping the clotting milk into the emptied bowls.

'The slugs love it. They even prefer it to lettuce. They climb into the bowls and drink till they're fat and bloated. They can't climb out again. They just quietly drown. They feel no pain.'

Elizabeth nodded. She was learning new things all the time.

She went to the rubbish heap and stared with interest at the mound of dead slugs there. It was very satisfying. 'No more eating lettuce for any of *you*,' she thought.

'It does make extra work, though,' sighed John, afterwards. Elizabeth noticed he looked rather tired. 'They say there's going to be a lot more wet weather next week. It's an extra job I could do without. That's what I was trying to explain to you, Elizabeth. That as soon as you stop having to water, there's a new job waiting to be done.'

They stood and looked at Elizabeth's lettuces, at the wreckage.

Elizabeth bit her lip, furious both with the slugs

and with herself. If only she'd stopped and listened to John, her lettuces might still be all right. To make matters worse, she had boasted about them, too. How the first form would laugh if they could see them now.

'You must ask for extra money at the next Meeting,' said John kindly. 'To buy new seeds with. It's not too late for a second planting. They would be ready by August.'

Elizabeth shook her head stubbornly. The next Meeting was a whole week away, August an eternity. It would be the summer holidays. Nobody would be here to see them! If she couldn't watch her *own* lettuces grow and flourish, she would just have to admire John's.

'I've got an idea, John!' she exclaimed suddenly. 'Let me look after *your* lettuces, instead. You've got far too many jobs to do. You look really tired lately. And now you've shown me how to get rid of the slugs—'

'No! Certainly not!' said John sharply.

The little girl was speechless. It was as though she had been slapped.

'Are you going back now, Elizabeth?' he asked, more gently. 'Could you take the jug back to Cook for me, please?'

'No! Take it yourself!' she cried rudely. 'Aren't you frightened I might drop it and break it?'

With that she raced off, boiling with rage.

John, her friend John, was telling her she was useless. Not for one moment was she to be trusted with his precious lettuces! She could have wept with anger.

She was still feeling upset, an hour later.

'Hello, Elizabeth! Where did you disappear to?' asked her friends, as she came into the common room.

It annoyed her that they all looked so cheerful and happy. They were building a castle out of playing cards.

'You're not supposed to use the best playing cards for doing that!' said Elizabeth, before she could stop herself. 'Only the old ones.'

'But it's more fun with these!' laughed Julian.

From the other end of the room, Arabella was listening.

'You're not a monitor any more!' she called out. 'Has it slipped your mind, Elizabeth?'

Elizabeth turned away. She didn't feel like being friendly and sociable this evening. Or being teased.

'I'm tired,' she said, truthfully. 'I'm going to have an early night.'

'Really!' said Arabella, later. 'Did you notice? Elizabeth's face was like a thundercloud. It must be because you made that little joke this afternoon, Patrick. About her not being important and not needing to come to watch the match!'

34

PATRICK MAKES A LITTLE JOKE

'Perhaps she's sulking because she's not a monitor any more!' suggested Rosemary.

'Do you really think so?' wondered Patrick.

Across the room, Julian got up, stretched and yawned.

'Don't be stupid,' he said. His eyes were mocking. 'Elizabeth's made of stronger stuff than that. It will be something else, I expect. There will be something else going on in her head.'

He smiled to himself. With Elizabeth, there nearly always was.

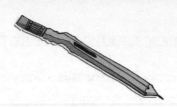

CHAPTER FOUR

JOHN TELLS ELIZABETH A SECRET

JULIAN WAS right, of course. Elizabeth went to bed that night still feeling cross about the slugs but even angrier that John had insulted her.

The following morning, in the dining-hall, she chose to ignore him.

'Good morning, Elizabeth,' he said, as they jostled to collect their cornflakes. 'Nice sunny one.'

Lower lip trembling slightly, she deliberately turned her back on him.

Back at her table, all the talk was about the tennis match against Woodville today.

'Isn't it lucky the weather's fine?' said rosy-cheeked Kathleen. 'Don't you think so, Elizabeth?'

Elizabeth said nothing. She could feel herself smouldering again. How could John behave as though nothing had happened?

Everybody noticed how quiet she was.

'I was only joking yesterday, Elizabeth,' Patrick said awkwardly, when breakfast was over. 'You will come

36

and watch the school match, this afternoon, won't you?'

Elizabeth nodded, hardly taking in what he was saying. Her mind was elsewhere.

'Of course, Patrick.'

Then, as she came out of the hall something unexpected happened.

She found John Terry lying in wait for her. He took her firmly by the arm.

'I've got to speak to you, Elizabeth.'

He propelled her round the corner, into the corridor, then gently pushed her into an empty classroom.

'Quick, in here. Nobody must hear.'

Elizabeth was too surprised to protest. Her bad feelings about John began to melt away. What was this all about? What did he want to say to her that was so important?

'Now look, Elizabeth,' he said, once the door was safely closed. 'I didn't mean to upset you last night. You must have thought me really rude and cruel. It was kind of you to offer to look after my plants. But I *had* to shut you up. I was frightened I might give something away.'

'Give something away?' asked Elizabeth, puzzled. But she was already feeling better, much better.

'Look, Elizabeth, can you keep a secret? A really important one. At least, it's important to me. There's not one person in the school knows. Nobody at all.'

Elizabeth began to feel excited and proud.

'Of course I can keep a secret!' she replied.

'Cross your heart and swear to die?'

Elizabeth did so.

'Right. Well, this is the position . . .'

Lowering his voice, he explained everything. He had filled in forms for a competition. He was hoping his two varieties of lettuce would win a very special cup at the Village Show. The Show was in two weeks' time, just before half-term. As well as medals for crafts and wood-working, there was a silver cup for the best produce grown by a young person under sixteen. It could be fruit, flower, plant or vegetable.

John was a modest boy. He was not doing this in the hope of personal glory. That was the last thing on his mind.

'If by any chance my lettuces win the cup, it will be a great honour for the school. The local people sometimes grumble about us and think we have a soft life. This would show them that we don't. That we're not afraid to get our hands dirty and work the soil and grow good things.'

'It would be in the local newspaper as well,' said Elizabeth, feeling excited. 'Then everybody would find out what a good school it is, and that we're allowed to do things for ourselves here . . .'

JOHN TELLS ELIZABETH A SECRET

She paused.

'But why must it be such a secret, John? I'd love to tell everyone—'

'Don't you dare!' he said fiercely. Suddenly Elizabeth realized just how important this was to him. He could not bear the idea of failing. Nor would he be able to bear it for everyone to *know* he had failed. 'If, by any chance, I pull it off and win the cup, I want it to be a *complete surprise*. Now promise again that you'll keep my secret.'

'I promise,' said Elizabeth, solemnly. 'I truly swear.'

'I've only told *you* because I wanted you to know why . . . last night . . . I wanted you to understand.'

'John, I'm so glad you have told me,' said Elizabeth. She looked ashamed. 'And I'm sorry I was so rude and hot-tempered. I do understand now. Of course you couldn't trust me to look after your plants, when it's so important—'

John looked at her in surprise. He interrupted her.

'Oh, Elizabeth, you still don't understand. I suppose I haven't explained properly. I *would* trust you to look after them. You're one of my best young helpers. You make mistakes sometimes, but you learn fast. No, it's not that.'

Elizabeth was beginning to feel a warm glow of happiness spreading through her.

'It's the competition rules,' he said. 'I've signed the entry forms and I had to vouch that whatever I grow will be my own, unaided work. Except for all the help Nature gives me, of course,' he added, smiling. 'Don't you see, Elizabeth? Nobody is allowed to help me with these lettuces in any way. Don't you dare even try to water them for me!'

As they emerged from the empty classroom and went their separate ways, Elizabeth wanted to laugh out loud with happiness. She had completely misjudged John. She had been silly and hot-headed and jumped to conclusions. Now everything was all right again. She was so pleased he had shared his secret with her. She would keep it safe.

Later that morning, Julian asked her to go out riding with him. He noticed how happy she seemed as they trotted along on their ponies, side by side.

'You were like a bear with a sore head earlier!' he remarked lightly. 'Was something the matter?'

'It was just a misunderstanding about something,' replied Elizabeth, cheerfully.

'Oh!' Julian smiled. 'I might have guessed.'

At Elizabeth's dinner table, all the talk was about the afternoon's match against Woodville. The visitors were due to arrive at two o'clock. The first formers were all proud that Patrick was playing in the second team.

'I've got to find my best form!' said Patrick edgily. He was feeling nervous. It was quite understandable. 'I did well in the trial. But if I play badly today it will be me out and Roger back in again!'

'We're all going to come and cheer you on, Patrick,' said Elizabeth.

After dinner, he left early to change into his tennis things. He now had a special badge sewn on his tennis shirt. It was a blue shield which showed that he was a second team player. He kept his precious tennis racket in a special place. He would collect that first before he changed. He was planning to get in a few practice strokes before the match.

The others sat around chatting in the dining-hall. They watched through the big windows as a minibus appeared in the drive.

'Here they come!' said Elizabeth. 'Watching this match is going to be fun.'

'Why are you in such a good mood, all of a sudden?' asked Arabella.

'Am I?' asked Elizabeth. 'Well, it's none of your business, even if I am.'

She stuck her tongue out at Arabella. Not being a monitor and having to set a good example had its compensations sometimes.

'Stop it, you two,' said Kathleen. 'Let's go and bag

places near the courts. We want to have a good view.'

Coming out of the dining-hall, they saw Patrick rushing towards them.

It was such a shock.

He hadn't changed yet. His black hair was completely dishevelled. His face was pale and distraught.

'My tennis racket!' he croaked. 'I've been looking for it everywhere. It's gone. Somebody must have taken it.'

CHAPTER FIVE

ELIZABETH IS ANGRY

PATRICK CONFRONTED Elizabeth. He was extremely agitated.

'Elizabeth, is this some kind of joke?' he asked. 'Have you hidden my racket? If you have, *please* give it back,' he pleaded. 'The match is starting in less than fifteen minutes.'

She stared at him in surprise.

'I don't know what you're talking about, Patrick,' she replied coldly.

'Of course she doesn't!' Julian scolded his cousin. 'As if Elizabeth would hide your racket—'

'What about the time she threw it in the bushes!'

'That was completely different,' replied Julian. 'Look, stop saying stupid things, Patrick. Try to think clearly. You must have mislaid it.' He added: 'If the worst comes to the worst, I'll lend you mine—'

'I don't want your silly old racket!' exploded Patrick. 'Mine's the only one I can play with properly. You know that perfectly well. I haven't mislaid it. It should be on

43

the top shelf in the sports cupboard. Everybody knows that's where I keep it. And it isn't there, I tell you!'

It was such an unexpected thing to happen. The first formers all gathered round him, feeling worried and surprised. They so wanted to see Patrick do well in his first match. They had been looking forward to it.

Meanwhile the two dark-haired, green-eyed cousins squared up to each other as if spoiling for a fight. Kathleen pushed the pair apart.

'Stop quarrelling, for goodness' sake. Let's all try and *do* something.'

'Yes, let's try and find Patrick's racket for him!' exclaimed Belinda.

Julian's anger at his cousin's rudeness suddenly passed. He could see how desperate he looked. He cooled down and took command of the situation.

'Patrick, dash and get changed,' he said, giving him a gentle push. 'You've only just got time! The rest of us will look for the racket. It can't be far away. I'm sure we'll find it.'

With a helpless shrug, Patrick strode off.

Julian organized a search party.

'Martin, while he's in the changing rooms you go and hunt around his dormy. He puts the racket under his bed sometimes, whatever he says. Kathleen, could you come with me? We'll search the sports cupboard.

ELIZABETH IS ANGRY

It might have slipped to the very back of the shelf. Elizabeth, would you go round to the south wall? He spends hours there, practising his strokes. He might have left it behind . . .'

Soon Julian had everybody rushing round the school, hunting for the missing racket, even some of the second formers.

Elizabeth was not quite so forgiving. She felt hot and bothered inside at the way Patrick had insulted her. How dare he suggest that she might play a joke on him, just before his important match? As if she would do something like that, even to her worst enemy.

Nevertheless, she hurried out of the building and made her way to Patrick's favourite spot. He loved to come here, near the shrubbery, and bang tennis balls against the wall, over and over again. Julian had a point. He might have left the racket behind last time.

She ran up and down, looking for it. She even hunted round the corner. But there was no sign of it.

She stared towards the bushes. Was it possible that Patrick had used it to search for a ball? The holly, for example, was very prickly. It was easier to part the leaves with one's racket than use one's hands.

Somewhere in the distance, she could hear children coming outside, calling to one another despondently.

'It's no use! It's definitely not in the building!'

'He must have left it outside somewhere. Let's look round the field!'

If Patrick *had* used the racket to find a ball, reasoned Elizabeth, perhaps something had distracted him. A school bell, even. He might have placed the racket on the ground, rushed off to lessons and then forgotten where he had left it. Well, it was a faint possibility.

She started to comb through the bushes, diligently.

There was still no sign of it.

She came out of the shrubbery, sucking her hand where the holly had pricked her. She stared across the school field towards the tennis-courts. The team from Woodville School had arrived. They were filing on to the court, carrying their tennis rackets. The fifteen minutes was up!

She saw Patrick, in his tennis whites. He was waiting by the entrance to the tennis-courts. He was staring at the ground, the picture of dejection. Elizabeth's heart went out to him. She could hear Julian shouting from a window somewhere—

'It's no use, Patrick. We can't find it. I'll bring my racket out for you. I'm just coming.'

Elizabeth slowly began to circle the school buildings. Rather than go across to watch the match, her eyes searched out every nook and cranny. This was beginning to look very suspicious.

ELIZABETH IS ANGRY

'I was cross with Patrick for talking to me like that,' she thought. 'But, in one way, he was right. Somebody *has* played a horrid joke on him. Somebody's taken his racket and hidden it somewhere. It's the only explanation. Otherwise, surely, one of us would have found it by now? Oh, poor Patrick!'

If only she could find it for him, thought Elizabeth, urgently. Her eyes scanned the big yard at the back of the school kitchens. It was out of bounds, but she crept in and searched around, even peering into some of the dustbins. Where would somebody hide a tennis racket? Not in a dustbin, surely? She was being silly. Where else? She walked through the yard and out into the back drive. She was standing by some parked cars. The Woodville minibus was parked round here, too.

There were garages beyond, most of them open.

'That might be a good place to hide a tennis racket,' decided Elizabeth. 'In one of the teacher's garages. No one would dream of looking in there. Besides, we're not allowed round here.'

Should she go and search them? The situation was desperate.

She looked left and right. There was nobody about. She started to tiptoe past the back of the nearest car. It was Miss Best's car, a rather old-fashioned blue saloon, with shining paintwork and chrome. Miss Best's car always looked immaculate.

'That's funny. She hasn't closed her boot properly!' Elizabeth realized. It was open several inches. She found it hard to imagine the joint headmistress being so careless. She would be leaving the car lights on next. 'I'd better close it for her.'

The little girl took hold of the chrome handle and tried to close the lid of the boot. It would not shut. There was something in the way. She opened the boot wider to see what the obstruction was—

It was a tennis racket.

She pulled it out and looked at it in amazement.

'It's Patrick's!' she gasped. 'How extraordinary.'

Somebody had tried to hide it in the boot of Miss Best's car.

'Well, they haven't succeeded!' she realized, joyfully.

Elizabeth slammed shut the boot. The noise brought Cook to the back door. 'What's Elizabeth doing here?' she wondered. 'I hope she's not being the Naughtiest Girl again.'

But Elizabeth had fled. With Patrick's racket in her hand, she ran all the way to the tennis-courts, her heart beating fast with excitement and triumph.

Patrick and his partner were at the far end of the first court, having a few practice strokes against the opposing pair from Woodville School. The match was

due to start in two minutes' time. Patrick looked a picture of misery as he fluffed a stroke with the borrowed racket. He was by now totally convinced that Elizabeth had hidden his own. Then he heard her voice.

'Patrick!' she shouted, through the wire netting. She was jumping up and down, waving the racket. 'I've found it!'

He raced off the court and came to meet her at the gate. Everybody was watching them.

'Oh, Patrick, isn't it lucky that I've found it in the nick of time?' she began, with a bright smile.

'Very funny, ha, ha. What a coincidence!' he hissed angrily.

He flung Julian's racket down at her feet and snatched his own. His face was like a thundercloud. The last few minutes had been the most miserable of his life. They had been almost unendurable.

'It's not amusing, Elizabeth,' he mouthed at her. 'I think you're beastly. I think this is the meanest trick I've ever come across.'

Elizabeth recoiled. She was speechless.

At that moment, atop the high green umpire's chair, Mr Warlow clapped his hands loudly.

'Time, please!' he called. 'Woodville won the toss and have chosen to serve. Back on court Patrick, please. Let the match begin.'

ELIZABETH IS ANGRY

Elizabeth slowly picked up Julian's racket and walked over to join the other first formers. Belinda and Kathleen had saved her a place on the big grassy bank that overlooked the courts. They slapped her on the back. So did Julian. He took possession of his racket with a wry smile.

'I don't think I'll lend it to *him* again in a hurry.'

'Where ever did you find it?' whispered Kathleen.

'In the boot of Miss Best's car,' replied Elizabeth, dully.

Belinda giggled out loud.

'The Beast's car boot? I don't believe it!'

Sitting just in front of them, Arabella turned her fair head scornfully.

'Don't tell fibs, Elizabeth Allen.'

'But it *was* in the boot of Miss Best's car,' Elizabeth hissed, fiercely. 'It was, it *was*. I looked inside and there it was!'

'You just *happened* to be passing the Beast's car and decided to *look inside the boot*?' asked Rosemary, in disbelief. She was sitting next to Arabella. 'You must have known it was there— You must have!'

'Seeing you'd hidden it there yourself!' suggested Arabella. She spoke primly. 'I think it was really mean to play a trick. And it's even meaner to pretend you didn't, now you feel scared. Now you see how serious it was.

You had half the school looking for that racket! If Patrick plays badly, it will be your fault, Elizabeth.'

'How dare you say that!' gasped Elizabeth.

'Please be quiet, children!' said Miss Ranger, their class teacher, who had just arrived to watch the match. 'You must not talk while play is in progress.'

Arabella studiously turned her well-groomed head away from Elizabeth and focused all her attention on the game. She clapped loudly every time Patrick won a point.

Far from playing badly, Patrick played a brilliant match. With his precious racket safely back in his hands, all his confidence returned. But there was something else. He was fired up with anger at the joke that he believed had been played on him. He turned all that anger into hard, fierce strokes, beating the pair on the other side of the net time after time. He would show Elizabeth Allen a thing or two! She would see what a fine player he was, not someone only fit to have tricks played upon them.

Elizabeth hardly noticed how well Patrick was doing. For it was her turn to feel miserable now. She sat through the match in a blur. She was seething with anger toward Patrick. For Arabella, with her sarcastic comments, she had only contempt.

Soon the match was over. Whyteleafe's second pair

had won by two sets to love! On the court, Patrick was elated. Eileen, his partner, was handing round one of the school biscuit tins. She was hospitality monitor for the day. At Whyteleafe, a different person was chosen to be hospitality monitor at every match. They were given the job of baking sweets, or biscuits, or little cakes, in the days before the match, to offer to all the players afterwards. Patrick was tucking into Eileen's fudge with relish.

He glimpsed the forlorn figure sitting on the bank. For the first time, he wondered if he could possibly have misjudged Elizabeth. It would be terrible if her 'find' had been genuine. He must ask the others about it.

A cheer suddenly went up. Whyteleafe's first team pair had won *their* match as well. Eileen quickly hurried over with the tin, to offer more fudge around. Both matches were over. Whyteleafe had won the fixture.

The news about Patrick's racket had quickly spread. Arabella was claiming that Elizabeth must be telling stories. She was pretending she had found the racket in the Beast's car boot! It was all too far-fetched. Elizabeth had been sulky after Patrick teased her about not being a monitor. She must have decided to get her own back, more likely. The whole thing had got out of hand, so now she was trying to wriggle out of it . . .

Noting the funny looks, Elizabeth's anger deepened.

'Don't worry. *We* believe you,' said Kathleen, sweetly.

But Elizabeth was scrambling to her feet. She had no intention of sitting round watching Arabella stir up mischief. She was even talking to Patrick now, as he came off court. She thought of the tremendous effort she had made to find his tennis racket for him. She had pricked herself. It was outrageous!

She strode away, heading back to school.

Julian caught up with her by the main doors. He grasped her arm.

'Elizabeth!' He grinned. 'Don't get in a huff. You must admit it sounds a tall story, about the car boot. If you and I weren't such good friends, I'm not sure I'd believe you myself.'

'Thanks!'

'You know what Arabella's like. I don't know why she has to stir things up so,' he said, becoming serious for once. 'I'm not sure anyone's taking her seriously.'

'Some of them are.'

'Only the silly ones.'

'Patrick thinks I hid his racket. He will be quite sure of it now.'

'Well, then, he's silly, too. What a chap to have as a cousin. He's an embarrassment sometimes. I'm beginning to wish all over again that he'd never come to Whyteleafe. I was beginning to enjoy myself.'

ELIZABETH IS ANGRY

'I hate him!' exclaimed Elizabeth.

Julian let go of Elizabeth's arm, put his hands in his pockets and frowned to himself. He turned over a small stone with the toe of his shoe. Then he looked her in the eye.

'The simple fact is, Elizabeth, that as you did *not* hide Patrick's racket in the boot of the Beast's car, somebody else did. But who? And why? I think we should go straight round to the car and have a hunt around. We need to look for clues.'

'I can't be bothered!' said Elizabeth, sulkily. 'If someone hates Patrick, it's no more than he deserves. Why should I care!'

'Except it would put you in the clear,' said Julian, calmly.

'I *am* in the clear!' exclaimed Elizabeth. 'I don't have to prove myself to people like Arabella and Patrick. My *real* friends know I wouldn't play such a silly, mean trick and that's good enough for me.'

At that moment some first formers appeared, Arabella amongst them.

Elizabeth turned her back on them and walked away.

She was tired of all this. She did not particularly want to see the rest of her classmates at the moment. Let them chatter away amongst themselves as much as they wished. She would go and do some gardening and enjoy some peace and quiet. She would go to the school gardens and find her dear John Terry and ask him to give her some jobs to do.

But, when she got there, there was no sign of him anywhere.

CHAPTER SIX

JULIAN LOOKS FOR CLUES

ELIZABETH WAS puzzled. She had never known John to be anywhere else but the school gardens on a fine Saturday afternoon. As well as the vegetable gardens, she looked for him in all the usual places: the greenhouses, the tool shed, the potting shed and round by the compost heap. He was nowhere to be found.

After looking for him all over she took a glance at his prize lettuces. They had grown some more and were hearting out nicely. She walked down the two rows, checking the bowls of milk. A few slugs had become trapped in them but there was plenty of room for more. At present, the soil having dried out well, the slimy black creatures had gone to ground. It would need another spell of wet weather to bring them out again in force. At the end of one row, a single dandelion was growing rather closer than it should to a cos lettuce. Elizabeth bent down to pull it out, then suddenly remembered.

She straightened up quickly. She had almost

forgotten. She must do nothing to help John's plants before the competition for the cup, in two weeks' time. No, not even pull out a single weed! It was against the rules. She was proud to be the only person in the whole school who knew John's exciting secret.

'Peter! Sophie! Have you seen John?' she called, as two junior class pupils appeared, carrying little forks and trowels.

'No,' replied Peter. 'Thomas is in charge today.'

'We're going to help put new straw round the tomato plants,' explained Sophie. 'The old straw got all wet. But first we're going to weed round the peas.'

The senior boy appeared then with the wheelbarrow laden with straw.

'That's the trouble when it's been wet,' laughed Thomas. 'It brings on the weeds faster than the things you're really *trying* to grow, don't you think, Elizabeth?'

'Yes.' Not to mention slugs and snails and other undesirables, Elizabeth thought. 'But, Thomas, what's happened to John today? I've been looking for him everywhere.'

'Haven't you heard?'

The big boy stood the wheelbarrow down and walked over to her.

'He's stuck away in the san, poor chap. He's got

German measles or scarletina or something, I've forgotten what. But it's very infectious! He's in a room on his own. Nobody's allowed to go anywhere near him, in case the whole school catches it.'

'Oh, poor John,' Elizabeth gasped.

'It's all right, it's nothing serious. He'll be completely better in a week or ten days. Then Matron will let him out!'

Elizabeth digested the dramatic news. She remembered how tired John had looked the other evening; it must have been because the illness was coming on.

'Until he's let out of San, I'm in charge of the school gardens,' said Thomas proudly. 'And by the way, John gave Matron a message to give me. Nobody is to go near his private patch or touch any of his plants. Strictly forbidden.'

Elizabeth nodded. She knew the reason for that!

Her mind had already turned back to John's lettuces. She glanced at the sky, feeling anxious. A week or ten days! That was such a long time. Supposing it got very wet again and more slugs appeared and needed to be attended to? Or supposing there was a heat wave, with long, hot days and the plants became parched and needed to be watered?

It did not bear thinking about.

'Have you come down to help?' Thomas was asking. 'Would you like to weed some peas, with Sophie and Peter?'

'Oh, please come and help us, Elizabeth,' said Sophie, running over and taking her hand. 'Look how many weeds have grown!'

Elizabeth smiled. 'I'll enjoy that, Sophie!'

After an hour's gardening, Elizabeth felt much better. There was something deeply relaxing about working with the soil, in the gentle sunshine, the sights and sounds and smells of nature all around. It was impossible to feel anxious for long as one listened to the doves cooing in the dovecote, the bees buzzing round the wallflowers.

The following day at breakfast she was pleased to see through the windows that it was another mild day. Would the weather continue like this for the next ten days? With gentle sunshine and just the occasional sharp shower, John's plants would be perfectly safe. Nature would take care of them for him, while he was locked away in the San.

That afternoon she went out riding with Julian again.

'I did go and look for clues yesterday, Elizabeth,' he told her airily. 'After you went off. I wandered over and had a good hunt round the Beast's car.'

They both reined in their ponies.

'Oh? Did you find anything?'

'Just this old crisp packet, blowing about under the car.' He produced a crumpled bag from the pocket of his jeans. It had stars and stripes on it and a picture of Uncle Sam. 'It's an American brand, *Southern Favorits*. Never heard of them, have you?'

Elizabeth glanced at the packet and shook her head.

'It could have blown over from the school dustbins. It doesn't mean anything.'

'True,' agreed Julian. He grinned. 'I've had a thought, though. Do you think the culprit could have been Roger Brown? Trying to upset Patrick, so he could get his place in the second team back?'

Elizabeth frowned and thought about the big, gentle senior boy. She simply could not imagine him creeping around and hiding Patrick's racket.

'Impossible,' she replied.

They looked at each other ruefully.

'In any case,' Elizabeth laughed. 'I'm not sure I care!'

The fact was that Elizabeth and Julian's cousin were no longer on speaking terms. They had simply decided to ignore each other. At the dinner table today, Patrick had been rather full of himself. There was to be another home match next weekend. Whyteleafe would be playing St Faith's and Patrick had been picked for the second team again. After his good performance against

Woodville, his place was beginning to look very secure.

'And Mr Warlow has asked me to be hospitality monitor,' Patrick told Martin, 'as a reward for playing so well. Isn't that an honour!'

'You were brilliant,' said Martin, who was now a great admirer.

'It will be quite a tough match,' said Patrick. 'But the *really* big match will be the one after that, just before half-term.'

'You mean the match against Hickling Green?' said Rosemary, knowledgeably.

Whyteleafe v. Hickling Green was always *the* big tennis fixture of the summer term. The two schools were long-standing rivals.

'Yes,' nodded Patrick. 'A lot of parents come to watch, if they're collecting us at half-term. I've got to play well against St Faith's, to make sure of my place for the big match.'

'I'm sure you will, Patrick,' cooed Arabella. 'Especially now you're keeping your racket safely locked up.'

Nobody else at the table had taken part in this conversation.

Unofficially the class was starting to divide into two factions.

There was a very small faction consisting of Patrick, Arabella, Rosemary and Martin. These four, together with one or two hangers-on, firmly believed that Elizabeth had played a mean trick on Patrick and was refusing to own up. She had not once been called the naughtiest girl in the school for nothing.

A much bigger faction, consisting of Julian, Belinda, Kathleen, and many others, sided firmly with Elizabeth. They felt sure that if by any chance Elizabeth had played a joke, as a former monitor (and such a fine one) she would certainly have owned up.

'As a matter of fact, Julian,' Elizabeth said now, as they turned their ponies to head back to school, 'I really do *not* care. I mean even if it *was* Roger wanting to get his place back in the second team. He deserves it more than Patrick does. He's much more decent than Patrick.'

'Yes.' Julian's green eyes twinkled. His friend was being illogical. 'Of course. And much too decent to have played such a trick in the first place. Well, Elizabeth,' he added airily, 'if you don't care, then why should I?'

There the conversation ended. They trotted briskly back to the school stables. After seeing to the pony, Elizabeth decided to wander down to the school gardens. She had a compulsion to keep an eye on John's project.

'I must just check that the plants are all right,' she thought. 'Even though there's nothing at all I can do about it, if they're not.'

The prize lettuces looked as fine as ever. No more slugs had appeared. The few in the bowls remained thoroughly bloated and drowned-looking.

'I suppose there's no chance they can somehow revive?' Elizabeth fussed to herself. 'It would be awful if they're just unconscious and could come back to life again.'

She walked round to the small rubbish heap where John had dumped all the dead creatures before. There was quite a mound of them. She turned them over with a twig, one by one, examining each one carefully. At first she screwed up her nose but she soon got used to them. Poor fat things!

'Yes, they're dead all right,' she thought. 'They're as dead as doornails. So the milk idea really, really works . . .'

'*UGH!*' came a voice at her shoulder.

Elizabeth sprang to her feet guiltily. She turned round.

Sophie was standing right behind her. The child's eyes were round as saucers.

'Why are you playing with those dead slugs, Elizabeth?' she asked, with a shudder.

Elizabeth hurriedly threw the twig away and laughed.

'It's my secret hobby, Sophie!' she joked, 'I like playing with dead slugs.'

'Do you really?' asked the child, solemnly. She had been watching for some time.

'Look here, Sophie,' said Elizabeth briskly. She took her firmly by the hand. 'You know you're not allowed to come wandering down here on your own.'

'I just wanted to look at all the flowers again. They do smell lovely.'

'Well, you're coming back to school with me, right now.'

Sophie was reluctant to leave the flowers. Elizabeth decided to cheer her up.

'I'll teach you a funny song,' she said kindly. 'It's one my governess told me. You can make up any names you like to put in it.'

Soon they were chanting it together, all the way back to school:

What is little Sophie made of? What is little Sophie made of?
Sugar and spice and all things nice
That's what little Sophie is made of!
What is little Patrick made of? What is little Patrick made of?
Slugs and snails and puppy dogs' tails
That's what little Patrick is made of!

At the main doors, they parted, with peals of laughter. Sophie liked the song. She would use it for skipping!

Elizabeth felt cheerful, too. She loved being at Whyteleafe School, in spite of the fact that she was no longer a monitor. She and Julian had been for such a good ride. And John's lettuces were looking fine. They were looking better than ever.

But the next day, the rains came back.

CHAPTER SEVEN

ELIZABETH MAKES UP HER MIND

'WILL YOU please be so kind as to stop staring at me, Elizabeth?' requested Mam'zelle during French, the first lesson on Monday morning. 'Will you be so kind as to keep your eyes down and fixed on your work? Do you not know it is very rude to stare? What is the matter with you this morning? Is it that you have never before seen a person eating a biscuit?'

From the rest of the class there came muffled giggles as the boys and girls glanced up from their vocabulary sheets.

'Sorry, Mam'zelle,' Elizabeth apologized. 'I wasn't really staring at you. I was thinking about something else.'

'You will think about your French vocabulary while you are sitting in my lesson, if you please, Elizabeth.'

Elizabeth lowered her head obediently. She pored studiously over her word sheet. Mam'zelle had given them ten minutes to learn some vocabulary while she herself marked some second form essays over by the big window. Then there would be a test.

Elizabeth had not even noticed that Mam'zelle was eating a biscuit, it was such a commonplace. The temperamental French teacher carried her school biscuit tin everywhere, full of Cook's home made oatmeal biscuits. She needed them, she had explained to Miss Belle and Miss Best, to counteract the nervous dyspepsia she suffered when taking lessons. It helped to keep her digestive system calm. Everybody knew that. So naturally, first thing on Monday morning out had come the biscuit tin.

'I wish they would keep the *rest* of her calm,' Elizabeth sighed to herself. She was embarrassed to have received a scolding in front of the whole class.

The little girl had been staring not at Mam'zelle but at the window panes beyond. There were large raindrops splattering on to them. Drip-drop. Drip-drop. They were getting louder and larger by the minute. Elizabeth had found it difficult not to watch the rain. Was this just the beginning or would it soon stop?

The rain did not stop. It poured down relentlessly until the middle of the afternoon.

'This will bring the slugs out again, for sure,' Elizabeth thought, in despair. 'And with none of us able to do a thing about it.'

She now felt deeply anxious about John's project once again. The glimmerings of a plan began to form in the back of her mind.

After tea that day, when the rain had stopped, she walked down to the village with her friend, Joan. The children were only allowed to go to the village in pairs.

'What are you going to buy at the shops today, Elizabeth?' asked the second former.

'I'm going to get some sweets for John Terry,' she replied. She still had fifty pence left, even after paying Belinda back for some stamps she had borrowed. She had been planning to save the fifty pence but this was more important. 'John must be so miserable on his own in the san, day after day.'

'You are a very kind person, Elizabeth,' said Joan quietly, linking arms with her best friend as they walked along. 'Susan thinks so, too.'

'Susan?'

'Yes. William and Rita told her how you stood down as an honorary monitor, so that she could have a proper turn. I was so proud of you when I heard that. You were being such a fine monitor.'

Elizabeth felt noble again. Then, she suddenly blushed.

'Oh, Elizabeth, you've gone all red!' laughed Joan. 'I didn't mean to embarrass you.'

'It's not that,' confessed Elizabeth. 'The fact is, I'm quite pleased I'm *not* a monitor at the moment. I'm planning to do something rather un-monitorish. I wish I could explain to you but I can't. It's to do with somebody else's secret, you see.'

'Try not to get into any scrapes, then. But I am sure you will have a good reason, for whatever it is you are planning to do.'

'I have got a good reason,' Elizabeth told herself an hour later, as she crept through the grounds towards the school sanitorium. John's sweets were in her hand. 'I only hope his room is one of the ground floor ones. And I only hope Matron doesn't see me!'

Unluckily for Elizabeth, the very first window she peered through found her looking straight into Matron's face!

Matron was sitting at her desk in her office and she looked up in surprise when she heard a rustle of bushes. Then she saw Elizabeth's face at the window. She quickly opened the window wide and leaned out.

'Goodness gracious, Elizabeth Allen, you gave me such a scare!' she exclaimed. 'What are you doing, creeping round here like a burglar?'

Elizabeth was mortified.

'I wanted to give John a wave through his window but I didn't know which room,' she said hurriedly. 'I was going to wave these sweets at him to cheer him up. I went and bought them for him after tea.'

'You won't be waving through any window at John for a while, you silly girl. He's upstairs and he's tucked up in bed fast asleep. He has to stay in complete isolation you know, Elizabeth. Just until the rash has gone and his temperature's back to normal.'

However, Matron took the sweets for him. Before closing the window on Elizabeth she spoke much more gently.

'Everybody knows John's in quarantine! But you've got a good heart. It *will* cheer him up to know someone's come over with some sweets. He's been a real misery today, I can tell you. Fussing on about the rain and his blessed garden. A drop of rain, I ask you! It must be the fever, I expect.'

Elizabeth slipped away feeling worse than ever. Her plan had come to nothing. Poor John! She had been so hoping she might get the chance to talk to him through the window. To tell him she thought that the competition rules were plain silly now and he must be prepared to let her help him a little bit. But she had been caught by Matron straight away!

Her feet began to drag as she struggled with her conscience for a while.

It was very difficult to come to a decision. But it was

the thought of John lying on his sick bed, fretting and unhappy, that finally persuaded her.

'John's so great – I've got to help him. The competition rules *are* silly now. I've got to look after his plants for him, without his knowing. And without anybody else knowing, either. Nobody need *ever* know, not even John himself!' she realized. 'All that will happen is he'll still win the special cup for the school, just as he's always hoped!'

Elizabeth broke into a run. Her mind made up, there was no time to lose. Recklessly, she ran immediately across to the school kitchens and found Cook.

'A jug of milk, Elizabeth? Whatever do you want a whole jugful for?'

'Oh, drat!' thought Elizabeth.

Then, looking through the side windows, she saw Fluff, the school cat, sitting outside on the low wall.

'I think Fluff looks thirsty,' she said, not untruthfully.

'Fluff always looks thirsty,' laughed Cook. 'Well, you're not going to give him a whole jugful. I'll pour some in a bowl for you.'

She found an old bowl under the middle sink and filled it from a jug.

'Off you go. And when you see Patrick could you give him a message? Tell him I shall have some more cooking chocolate on Thursday, if he wants to make his crispy cakes then.'

Elizabeth slipped out of the side door, walked straight past Fluff and headed for the school gardens. She carried the bowl carefully, for Cook had been generous. She did not notice Fluff stretch, yawn and decide to follow her.

'I don't suppose this will be nearly enough, but at least it's a start,' thought Elizabeth, eagerly. She glanced around, anxious not to be seen.

Luckily the grounds were deserted.

In fact, it was getting so late that Elizabeth should have been indoors. This was the time of evening when the first formers were expected to read or play quietly in the common room.

'I wonder what's happened to Elizabeth?' Belinda was saying. 'I haven't seen her.'

'Perhaps she has a piano lesson,' shrugged Julian, in his casual way.

'No, that isn't today,' said Kathleen.

'If you ask me,' Arabella intervened, 'Elizabeth is not exactly sociable these days. It's the shock of not being a monitor any more, I suppose.'

'*If* we ask you, we will be very interested to hear what you have to say,' replied Julian. 'But as we haven't asked you, we are not.'

Elizabeth tiptoed through the school gardens and

found John's vegetable patch. The ground was squelchy. She placed the bowl of milk carefully on the path and went to examine his salad plants.

It was such a relief to be doing something positive at last. From the moment she had made the decision to help John in secret, a weight had lifted from her mind. There was nothing worse than sitting around, worrying and feeling helpless. This was going to be much more fun.

Half expecting to see the hearty green leaves ravaged by slugs, as her own had been, she was cheered to find them still intact.

She smiled as she thought of what Cook had said about Patrick and the cooking chocolate. Patrick had been going around saying it was sissy to have to make sweets or something, just because he was to be hospitality monitor at the St Faith's match on Saturday. A girl ought to make them and let him have the honour of handing them round. Even Arabella had drawn the line at that. In that case, he boasted, he would get hold of some of those biscuits like Mam'zelle's. But secretly he was making something, after all!

Well, it would be difficult for *her* to give him the message. They were still not speaking. She would have to ask one of the others to tell him.

Elizabeth's mind turned back to the slug situation.

ELIZABETH MAKES UP HER MIND

Looking in the six bowls, one by one, she found that a lot more slugs were now trapped in them. The soil was very wet after today's rain and this had brought them out again.

'Two of the bowls are nearly full!' she realized. 'Although the other four are all right.'

How lucky that she had got some milk from Cook straight away. There would be just enough to sort out the two nearly-full bowls. Screwing up her nose, she carried them both over to the little rubbish pile and tipped them out on to the waiting slug mound. That was goodbye to some more fat slugs!

She came back, bent down and replaced the empty bowls in position.

'Now to get the milk and tip half in each,' she thought. Then she stopped. As she had straightened up, she had felt something rubbing against her legs. There came a loud purring sound.

She looked down.

'Fluff!' she exclaimed. Then she saw the traces of milk on his mouth and whiskers. 'Oh, no!' squealed Elizabeth.

She ran over to find her milk.

The bowl was empty.

The big cat with the fluffy face had drunk every last drop.

Elizabeth trudged back to the school kitchens with the empty bowl, feeling a sense of despair. Why did things have to go wrong? She had tried to help John but in fact she had made matters worse. There had been six working slug traps and now there were only four. She had put two of them out of action. As those two bowls were now empty, the creatures would just ignore them. The four remaining bowls would not suffice very much longer. Given more rain, John's lettuces would soon be getting devoured! Oh, what should she do now?

The kitchens were deserted. Cook and her helpers had finished for the day. All the washing up had been done, the floor swabbed down. Elizabeth crept over to the middle sink, carefully washed and dried the old bowl, then replaced it in the cupboard below. About to leave, she noticed that someone had carelessly left the pantry door ajar. She walked over to close it. It was a beautifully cool room, with a stone-flagged floor and marble shelves. Staring inside, Elizabeth glimpsed a long row of large jugs, each with a little square of muslin draped over the top.

On an impulse she slipped in, and peered inside the nearest jug.

It was full of milk. They all were. It was the milk for the children's breakfast cereal. As it was cool this evening, one of Cook's helpers had set them up in readiness for the morning.

'Tons and tons of milk!' realized Elizabeth. She picked up the near jug. It was quite heavy. 'Oh, nobody would ever miss one jug, would they? Not just one!'

It was a reckless thing to do. It was very hot-headed of Elizabeth.

She left with the jug, stealing along the corridors as quickly as she could without spilling the milk inside. She would hide the big jug in her bedside locker!

As she turned a corner, she paused. The common-room door was wide open and she would have to pass it before she could get up the stairs.

The only thing she could do was to make a dash for it!

'Elizabeth!' her friends cried, as she flashed by.

They crowded to the door, only to see her back view disappearing upstairs.

'Aren't you coming in?' they shouted.

'I'm sleepy, I'm going to bed!' came the muffled reply.

A minute later, she was on her knees in the dormitory by her bedside locker. She cleared a space for the jug of milk, placed it inside, then closed the cupboard door. Nobody ever looked in people's lockers. They were private.

To get her breath back, she flung herself on the bed and lay staring at the ceiling.

'What have I done?' she thought, feeling surprised at herself. 'Well, there's no going back now.'

Slowly, very slowly, a feeling of relief crept over her. It could rain as much as it liked this week. The slugs could come marching out if they wanted to. She had plenty of ammunition now. She would be ready for them!

But as so often happens in the scheme of things, there *was* no more heavy rain that week! The ground dried out nicely. Weather conditions for growing prize lettuce turned out to be quite perfect!

Elizabeth continued to keep a watchful eye on them and was thankful. Great secrecy and stealth would have been required, to help them along. Roger, no longer in the tennis team, was always working in the gardens these fine evenings, as was Thomas.

The large jug of milk remained hidden in her locker, untouched and, in time, forgotten.

So when a second former stood up at the next school Meeting, her words gave Elizabeth a shock.

'Please, I have a complaint. On Tuesday morning, when our table went up to collect our jug of milk, there was none left. Cook said staff always fill the right number of jugs, so one table must have been greedy and taken two. We had to share a jug with the next table and we all had a measly amount of milk on our cornflakes. I think the table that took two jugs of milk ought to own up.'

William and Rita, as Judges, looked around the crowded hall.

'Did any table help themselves to an extra jug of milk on Tuesday morning?' asked Rita pleasantly. 'If so, would they please own up now?'

There was silence.

The head boy and girl waited patiently for a few moments. There were rows of blank faces. It was obvious that no one was going to stand up.

At a nod from Rita, William looked relieved and banged the gavel on the little table.

'Very well,' he announced, with a smile. 'I think on this occasion we can be quite sure that one of the kitchen staff *did* make a little mistake. None of us is perfect! You must put the matter behind you, Chloe, and not be the last table to collect its milk next time!'

The whole school laughed.

Elizabeth felt very hot. As soon as the Meeting ended, she had to rush outside and gulp in some fresh air.

She had never in her life not owned up to something before. She felt terribly guilty. But how could she explain to the Meeting about the missing jug of milk without giving John's secret away?

She went for a walk in the grounds, to calm herself down.

Meanwhile, in the dormitory she shared with some of the other girls a mystery was being investigated.

'I've noticed the funny smell for days,' said Jenny. 'But it's suddenly much worse. It's really bad today.'

'It seems to be coming from Elizabeth's locker!' exclaimed Belinda, sniffing around. 'Do you think we ought to look inside? I'm sure she wouldn't mind.'

When Elizabeth entered the dormitory, she found a crowd of girls waiting for her. Belinda was holding a large, empty milk jug in her hands. She had washed all the sour milk down the sink.

'So someone did take a jug of milk, after all,' said Jenny. 'And it was you, Elizabeth. What did you take it for? It had all gone sour. You hadn't even drunk any!'

Elizabeth just stared at the empty jug in dismay and said nothing.

'Why didn't you own up at the Meeting?' asked Kathleen, looking upset.

'We've stuck by you all this time, Elizabeth!' exclaimed Belinda, who felt betrayed. 'But is it true what some people have been saying? That you do things and don't own up to them. That you can't be bothered to be good now you're not a monitor any more?'

'*Please* explain,' begged Kathleen.

'I can't explain, Kathleen!' Elizabeth blurted out. 'I just can't.'

Rosemary was standing in the doorway listening.

'Arabella has been right about you all along!' she said smugly.

Elizabeth rushed past her and away down the corridor. She was feeling confused and upset.

She had done something wrong. Now she had been found out.

Even Belinda and Kathleen and Jenny were starting to turn against her.

But she had only been trying to keep a secret.

She was thankful that the weekend lay ahead and she would not have to face the whole class again before Monday. She would spend some time with Joan.

First, in the morning, she would have a private talk with Julian.

CHAPTER EIGHT

A PRIVATE LETTER ARRIVES

JULIAN WAS full of good advice the next morning.

'You're in a tight corner, Elizabeth, all because of this silly secret!' he said. 'Whatever is it? Has someone been asking you to make them some cheese? You can't keep that secret for long, it makes such a pong!'

His green eyes were laughing and full of mischief. Everything happened to Elizabeth!

'Of course not,' she replied. 'And if they were, I wouldn't be able to tell you. But it's something much more important than that. And I've crossed my heart and sworn to die.'

'I know that. And so you can't go and confess to William and Rita, which is what the whole class expects you to do,' smiled Julian, wryly. 'Even if you *could* confess, it wouldn't help much. The damage is done!'

'I know,' nodded Elizabeth. 'Now everybody thinks that I played that trick on Patrick. That I hid his racket and was scared to own up about that, as well. That's the thing I can't bear!'

'It's known as giving a dog a bad name,' said Julian. He patted her brown curly hair. 'Oh, poor bad, bold girl. Woof! Woof!'

'It's not funny,' protested Elizabeth. 'I didn't mind it when only two or three people sided with Patrick but now *everyone* does. And the way Patrick looked at me this morning! I don't think he was *really* sure that I hid his racket, it was just Arabella winding him up. But now he's convinced!'

'Isn't it about time we found out who really did?' asked Julian quietly.

'Yes!' agreed Elizabeth. 'And I'm sorry, Julian. I didn't take it seriously before. I was proud and silly. I was just so cross, that's all. To think I was the one who had gone to all that trouble and *found* his beastly racket for him! But now I see I *do* have to put myself in the clear over that. It might even be – well – nicer for Patrick, too,' she admitted, ruefully. 'Oh, poor Patrick.'

Julian had very little time for his cousin but now he looked thoughtful.

'Yes. I suppose so. He *was* pretty upset that you didn't come and watch his tennis trial. Then he must have thought you really disliked him – enough to play a mean trick just before his first match. Not very nice for him. I hadn't really thought about it much from

Patrick's point of view,' he admitted, airily.

'Nor me,' agreed Elizabeth.

She tried to concentrate hard. She thought of the crisp packet Julian had found, *Southern Favorits*.

'Arabella's parents are in America,' she said, tentatively. 'That's why she's come to Whyteleafe. You don't think it's possible they send her goodies, like crisps and things?'

'She never hands them round, if they do,' frowned Julian. 'Besides, where's the motive? We have to find a motive.'

'Well, maybe to get me into trouble,' suggested Elizabeth.

'But she could never have planned it that *you* would find the racket!'

'Maybe that was just a bonus?' sighed Elizabeth.

'The whole thing seems too imaginative for Arabella,' Julian replied rather drily. 'Still. Interesting about her parents being in America. I didn't know that. Would you like to search her dormy?'

'Yes. This afternoon!' nodded Elizabeth. 'While she's safely at the match!'

Elizabeth had already decided not to watch the match against St Faith's this afternoon. She preferred to avoid her classmates at present. It was too horrid, the looks she was starting to get. She had arranged to go to the village with Joan, instead. But Arabella would be at the match, no doubt sitting in the front row.

'The perfect opportunity!' agreed Julian, as they walked back to school together.

'I'll look in her desk, as well,' said Elizabeth, excitedly. 'What will you do, Julian?'

'I shall be at the tennis match,' replied Julian, casually. 'Watching points.'

When she returned indoors, Elizabeth found an envelope in her pigeon-hole. It was firmly sealed and marked *Elizabeth Allen PRIVATE*.

She ran along to the girl's cloakroom and locked herself in a cubicle. Then she opened the envelope to see what was inside.

It was a note from John Terry. He had smuggled it out of the san with the help of one of the school cleaners!

Dear Elizabeth,

Thanks for the sweets. I am feeling much better and have enjoyed them. I shall be out of my 'prison' in a few more days, just in time for that IMPORTANT THING I am going to do. But I am dead worried. It says on the radio there will be heavy rain from Monday onwards. Please keep a close eye next week. Remember do NOT do anything to help them along or

86

we will break the rules. But I have an important job for you.

If they start getting attacked, please dig the very best specimens out of the ground. Wrap them in newspaper and hide them in the potting shed. There is a big, cool cupboard in there on the north-facing wall. Do NOT let anyone see you or they will ask questions. Thank you, special helper . . .

Your grateful friend

JOHN

P.S. When you have read this note, destroy it completely.

Elizabeth carefully memorized the note. Then with trembling fingers, she tore it in into tiny pieces, dropped it down the lavatory pan and flushed it clean away.

It was so exciting to have received a secret message from John. Now she could only feel grateful that all her efforts to help the plants along had come to nothing. No rules had been broken, after all. John would have been angry, if he had ever found out.

But at last, with the lettuces almost ready to pull, he had given her a very important job to do. He was placing his trust in her to do it well. After that, he would soon be back in charge again, thank goodness. He would take his prize lettuces to the village show and win the cup and bring honour to the school! She took her place at dinner with her head held high.

Patrick and Eileen won their match again, although it was a much closer result than against Woodville, the week before. As Patrick proudly handed round his chocolate crispy cakes to the visitors from St Faith's, Miss Ranger and her class clapped and cheered loudly.

'Oh, well done, Patrick!' shouted Arabella. She turned to Julian. 'Wasn't your cousin marvellous?'

'Was he?' asked Julian.

He had not been following the rallies closely.

He had spent most of the time studying the spectators, watching one face in particular.

Elizabeth, meanwhile, had found nothing of interest amongst Arabella's things.

She had been shocked to see how many clothes and pairs of shoes the spoilt little rich girl had smuggled back to school this term, even though it was against the rules. They were hidden under her bed. But of packets of American crisps, or indeed anything American, there was no sign.

'I'd feel rather sorry for her, if I didn't dislike her so much,' thought Elizabeth, her searches completed. She felt guilty for prying, now. 'It must be horrid being the oldest in the class and nearly always coming bottom and having your parents so far away.'

She went off to meet Joan and go to the village. She was lucky to have such a real and special friend, she decided. Arabella's friend Rosemary was very weak and just toadied to her.

Later she said to Julian:

'I'm afraid I drew a blank. How about you?'

'I spent most of the match watching Roger Brown's face,' replied Julian. 'And he looked pretty miserable, even when Patrick and Eileen were winning. It was written all over his face, even when his hands were clapping!'

'Upset to see Patrick playing well again? But that would be only natural,' mused Elizabeth. 'He must be secretly hoping to get his place in the team back. It's the big match next week against Hickling Green, when lots of parents come. He might have wanted to play in that and now it looks like being Patrick again.'

'I agree,' said Julian. 'It certainly doesn't prove he's done anything wrong.'

Neither of them wanted to think that about Roger.

'All the same,' sighed Julian, 'I think we should try and keep an eye on him.'

By Sunday night, Elizabeth remembered there was something else she would need to keep an eye on. This time, with John Terry's permission.

It had started to rain again.

It rained all that night and when they trailed into French on Monday morning, it was still raining.

'The lettuces have been doing so brilliantly,' thought Elizabeth. 'But there's still time for them to be ruined. I may have to start pulling them by tomorrow. I'll go down and have a look at them after tea today. Even if I have to take my umbrella with me!'

But Elizabeth never got the chance.

Something terrible happened in the French lesson that morning, something truly amazing.

They were all sitting at their desks, their heads bent over their books as they copied down a passage from the blackboard. Mam'zelle quietly opened her biscuit tin and slid her hand inside to pull out her first biscuit of the week, then—

'*Aaaaagh*!'

She screamed, and dropped the tin.

She had pulled out a handful of dead slugs.

CHAPTER NINE

THE MEETING DECIDES
TO PUNISH ELIZABETH

MAM'ZELLE LEAPT to her feet, flinging the slugs away in horror. One hit Arabella on the nose and she screamed as well. The tin had clattered noisily to the floor, scattering dead slugs everywhere and a few snails, too.

The classroom door was flung open and Miss Belle appeared.

'Whatever's the matter—?'

'This is the matter, very very *very* much the matter!' cried Mam'zelle, picking a slug off her skirt and holding it at arm's length, between thumb and forefinger, before letting it drop to the floor with the others. 'Look what horrible things have been put in my tin. There are some very wicked children in this class. They think they make everybody laugh—'

Some of the class were indeed stuffing their fists in their mouths. The way Arabella had screamed! And Mam'zelle had looked so funny, holding up the slug like that . . .

One look from Miss Belle quelled their laughter. She was angry.

'Martin, go and find a school cleaner to come and clear up this mess at once for Mam'zelle. The rest of the class sit in silence.'

After Mam'zelle returned from washing her hands, Miss Belle gazed at the children for a few moments.

'Whoever was responsible for that silly trick is to come and own up at dinner-time. That will be all.'

The class was very subdued after that. Elizabeth frowned in deep puzzlement, wondering how the mound of slugs on John's rubbish heap could have found their way into Mam'zelle's biscuit tin.

Was there a practical joker at work? Had the same person hidden Patrick's tennis racket?

'Well, Roger can't have done this,' she whispered to Julian, at dinner-time. 'There's no possible motive!'

'And can you see Arabella dare even look at a slug? I can't!' Julian whispered back. He was as puzzled as Elizabeth.

Miss Belle, Miss Best and Mr Johns were puzzled, too. Nobody from the first form came to own up, as requested. The culprit must be elsewhere.

They asked the head boy and girl to call a special Meeting.

It took place immediately after tea, the same day.

THE MEETING DECIDES TO PUNISH ELIZABETH

'I hope the culprit owns up quickly,' whispered Belinda, as they filed into the hall. 'I want to play my new record in the common room.'

'I was hoping for a game of tennis but it's still raining,' said Kathleen. 'I wonder who managed to get into the kitchens and get their hands on Mam'zelle's biscuit tin? At least it doesn't seem to have been anybody in our class.'

'Unless it was another of Elizabeth's little jokes,' said Jenny, unhappily. 'And she's refusing to own up again.'

'Oh, I hope not,' said Belinda, biting her lip.

Of course, the rest of the form, especially Rosemary and Arabella, had been whispering about that possibility all day. Now they waited in keen anticipation to see what would happen at the Meeting.

Elizabeth was already in the hall, seated next to Julian. Her head was held high. She well knew what some of them were thinking but she was confident that the truth would come out at the special Meeting. She was impatient for it to start. After that she would get on with the important job of examining John's plants for him.

The school monitors were seated on the platform, with the head boy and girl. They all looked very serious. So did Miss Belle and Miss Best and Mr Johns, observing from the back of the hall.

The entire school was keyed up. A special Meeting was a rare event.

William banged the little hammer.

'I hope this matter can be dealt with quickly,' he told the assembly.

He explained, for the benefit of those who did not know (by now very few of them), exactly what had taken place during the first form French lesson.

He gazed around the hall, slowly and carefully.

'The simple fact is that *somebody* in this hall invented this foolish joke. It is quite unfair that the first form should be the only ones under suspicion. Rita and I therefore ask the person responsible to stand up now and own up. The Meeting will then decide what their punishment should be.'

He waited.

There was a breathless hush.

'Will the person please stand up?' he repeated.

He waited again. Still there was no movement in the hall.

William frowned. Then, quietly he consulted Rita and all the monitors. A minute later he came back and banged the gavel, to stem the tide of whispering in the hall.

'Silence, please. As you know, at Whyteleafe School we do not believe in tale telling. But if the person will not own up, we must get to the bottom of this in some other way. If anybody has any information, if they know anything at all that can shed some light on this, will they please stand up?'

Arabella could barely restrain herself, thinking of the previous incidents. She glanced at Patrick. But he gave a quick shake of the head and stared at the floor.

There then came a sound from the front of the hall. A member of the junior class, who had been sitting cross-legged on the floor, was scrambling to her feet. It was Sophie.

'What do you want to say, Sophie?' asked Rita, gently.

'I know where the person must have stolen the dead slugs from,' she said, importantly. 'They must have stolen them from Elizabeth.'

Elizabeth had a sinking feeling in the pit of her stomach. She could hear her classmates giving little gasps.

'From *Elizabeth*?' asked Rita.

'She's got a special place where she keeps them in the school garden,' explained Sophie. 'She likes playing with them sometimes, don't you, Elizabeth?' asked the child, in all innocence, at the same time turning round to look for Elizabeth.

'You may sit down now, Sophie,' said William.

'Elizabeth, stand up, please.'

Elizabeth did so, her cheeks aflame. Even Julian was looking at her in surprise.

'Is this true?' asked William. 'That you own some dead slugs?'

'I don't own them,' stated Elizabeth, her voice clear and decisive.

'But you know where there are some? You like playing with them?'

Some of the more senior pupils were snorting and trying not to laugh.

'I do know where there are some,' replied Elizabeth. 'But I don't really play with them. I was just messing about to see if they were properly dead.'

She stopped. If this line of questioning went on much longer, John's secret was bound to come out.

'Some of us might call that playing with them,' commented William.

Now the head girl stood up and took over.

'Elizabeth,' said Rita, gently. She was puzzled beyond belief. 'Please just answer one simple question. Yes or no. Did you put some slugs in Mam'zelle's biscuit tin?'

'No, Rita. I did not,' replied Elizabeth, in a loud, ringing voice. 'Somebody else must have found my slugs. That's what must have happened.'

That was too much for Arabella. She leapt to her feet.

'Fibber!' she cried indignantly. 'You must have done!'

'That will do, Arabella,' said William, firmly. 'If you have something to say, please address the whole Meeting.'

Arabella took a deep breath. But before she could compose a little speech, Patrick grabbed her arm.

'Shut up and sit down!' he hissed. 'You haven't any proof.'

Arabella subsided.

'Very well, then,' said William, looking troubled. 'The time has come for Rita and I to discuss things with the monitors and to come to a decision.'

Everybody on the platform went into a huddle. In the hall, the children whispered quietly amongst themselves. Julian gave Elizabeth's arm a squeeze.

'Don't they eat snails in France?' he grinned. 'Maybe that's why someone played the trick on Mam'zelle.'

'So what!' Elizabeth hissed back. She was in no mood for Julian's jokes. She was pent up, waiting to hear what the Meeting decided. She could see Joan up on the platform, speaking anxiously. She was quite sure that her best friend would be sticking up for her.

At long last, William returned to the table and banged the gavel.

'We have reached our decision. The two second form monitors are convinced that, whatever quarrels may be going on in the first form, Elizabeth Allen is very honest and has never been afraid to own up to wrongdoing. They know her best, of course, but Rita and I are of the same opinion. We have no evidence that Elizabeth played this trick and she has stated clearly to the whole Meeting that she did not. In due course we will discover the true culprit and until then let their own guilty conscience be their punishment.'

Elizabeth sighed with relief, proud to be a member of a school like Whyteleafe. But then her relief turned to dismay.

'Nevertheless, messing around with dead slugs is not something we would expect of a former monitor. It may even have given someone the idea for the trick played on Mam'zelle this morning. Please stand up again, Elizabeth. We have decided on your punishment.'

Elizabeth stood up, faced the platform and awaited her sentence.

'Until John Terry is released from the san and is able to supervise you again, you are forbidden from the school gardens. They are strictly out of bounds. That must be clearly understood.'

Elizabeth nodded and sat down. Her face was very pale.

THE MEETING DECIDES TO PUNISH ELIZABETH

The Meeting ended. Sophie was upset. She had not meant to get Elizabeth into trouble.

'If you ask me, you got off lightly, Elizabeth Allen!' scowled Arabella, as they came out of the hall. 'Who wants to do any gardening in this weather, anyway!'

'Yes, what a swizz!' echoed Rosemary.

Patrick was looking thoughtful. He hurriedly steered Arabella and her friend away from Elizabeth. He badly wanted to have a talk with them.

'Got off lightly?' thought Elizabeth, bitterly, as she stood and watched them go. She could have wept with frustration. She had been banned from the school gardens. She would never dare to defy such a ban, given out by the Meeting in front of the whole school. However unjust she knew it to be.

But it meant that she would be unable to follow John's secret instructions this week. She would be unable to save his prize lettuces for him. All the worry, all the trying to help, all the getting into trouble . . . it would all have been in vain.

The Meeting could not have decided on a worse punishment.

CHAPTER TEN

ARABELLA STIRS UP TROUBLE AGAIN

'COME ON, Rosemary. Let's go and talk to Cook,' said Arabella, the following afternoon. 'You never know, she might have seen something.'

'Do you really think we should?'

'Of course we should. I don't think Elizabeth should be allowed to get away with playing that trick on Mam'zelle! Patrick says we haven't got any proof. Well, let us see if we can find some!'

Arabella was still smarting, even twenty-four hours later, from the conversation that had taken place with Patrick.

The fact was that poor Patrick was rather confused.

He had been rather impressed with Elizabeth's bearing at the special Meeting, with the clearness and candour of her voice. He was sure she had played that mean trick with his tennis racket. He felt she must dislike him very much to have done that and the idea made him miserable.

ARABELLA STIRS UP TROUBLE AGAIN

But surely Elizabeth did not dislike Mam'zelle, too? They got on well. Why should she want to play an unkind trick on Mam'zelle? It did not make sense. At the special Meeting, she had seemed to Patrick like someone telling the truth. So could there be an anonymous joker on the loose in the school? Somebody with a rather warped sense of humour, who chose their victims at random? To someone like that, putting his racket in the boot of the Beast's car could have seemed really amusing.

Could it be, reasoned Patrick, that Elizabeth really *had* found his racket for him, in the nick of time, that day? The thought chastened him, remembering the bad things he had said to her. On the other hand, he found it strangely cheering. It would mean that Elizabeth did not dislike him, after all.

'What are you suddenly talking about proof for, Patrick?' Arabella had asked scornfully. 'Have you forgotten about the missing jug of milk? She didn't own up about *that* either. And it was actually found in her locker!'

Patrick had no answer. Yet he had still felt uneasy.

'Let's see what we can find out, Rosemary!' said Arabella, now. She felt excited as they walked over to the school kitchens together. She had discovered that Mam'zelle always left her empty biscuit tin with Cook at weekends, to be replenished for the new week ahead. 'Elizabeth could have got into the kitchens over the weekend and put her slugs inside the tin and shut the lid firmly. Then Mam'zelle could have come to collect her tin soon after. Picked up the tin, felt it was heavy and thought her biscuits were inside! Come to think of it,' frowned Arabella, 'I wonder what happened to the biscuits?'

'That's one of the things we can ask!' said Rosemary, who was not quite following all this.

Cook was on tea break but one of the kitchen helpers, Molly, was there.

'No, I didn't see nobody suspicious, not over the weekend,' she said blankly.

Then Rosemary asked if she had seen any of Mam'zelle's special oatmeal biscuits lying around anywhere.

'Well, isn't it funny you should ask that?' replied Molly, looking unhappy. 'I found them all dumped in the waste bin on Saturday afternoon. I don't think Mam'zelle could have liked the look of them this week. Very wasteful, I thought it was.'

In the waste bin!

'Are you *sure* you didn't see somebody from our form in here, on Saturday?' begged Arabella. 'Some time earlier? Before it was time for Mam'zelle to come to collect her tin? Think hard, Molly!'

'Well, only Patrick, of course,' said Molly. 'He came in to collect the tennis tin. He had made some nice chocolate crispy cakes for the tennis match. It was stood on the table, next to Mam'zelle's. I nearly gave him the wrong one. It's a blue tin, you see, very like hers.'

Arabella gasped out loud. Two blue tins. Of course!

'Thank you, Molly,' she said. 'You've been most helpful. If they didn't take all our money away from us at this school, I would give you a small gift.'

Then, grabbing Rosemary by the hand, she hurried out of the kitchens.

'Where are we going, Arabella?'

'To find Patrick, of course!' cried Arabella, triumphantly.

The rain had stopped for a while. They found Patrick by the south wall, practising his tennis strokes. Arabella was careful not to show her true feelings.

'Patrick, I'm afraid I've got some rather unpleasant news,' she said, sorrowfully.

She told him about the inquiries they had made in the school kitchens.

'So I'm afraid the slugs weren't meant for Mam'zelle, at all, Patrick,' she said, her eyes cast down demurely. 'The person dumped the biscuits and replaced them with slugs because they thought it was the tennis tin. They were playing a mean trick on *you* again, Patrick. Nobody would dare play a trick like that on Mam'zelle.'

Patrick's face turned pale, as the words sunk in.

A vivid picture of how it would have been came to his mind's eye. He, the hospitality monitor, proudly opening the blue tin, proudly offering round to the visiting team from St Faith's . . . the dead slugs! Elizabeth, sitting on the bank, waiting eagerly for this moment. Convulsed with laughter when she saw him humiliated . . .

So Elizabeth really did dislike him then. How he had fooled himself!

The sense of disappointment turned to a sudden rush of blind anger.

'And nobody will dare play a trick like that on *me* again, either!' he raged. 'Especially not Elizabeth Allen. Just wait till I find her.'

He pushed the two girls aside almost rudely and went racing round to the front of the school. Rosemary felt a twinge of anxiety. What was going to happen now?

It was very unfortunate.

Elizabeth was standing at the top of some steps outside the main doors. She was standing on one leg, like a stork, staring into space and thinking about John's lettuces. They were probably being chewed up right now, one by one, and there was nothing she could do . . .

Patrick came round the corner of the building, saw Elizabeth, then charged towards the steps, with his head down like an angry bull. He almost cannoned into Mr Johns on the way. He came bounding up the steps towards Elizabeth, shouting wildly and waving his arms—

'Those slugs and snails were meant for me, weren't they, Elizabeth! You wanted to make me look an idiot. You wanted to get me into trouble—'

His flailing arms caught Elizabeth's right elbow and she overbalanced. With a cry of surprise she found herself slithering all the way down the steps, to crash face downwards into a big muddy puddle at the bottom. She lay there, winded, gasping for breath. Whatever was the matter with Patrick? It had all been a dreadful shock.

Miss Ranger came running over. Both she and Mr Johns helped the girl to her feet. Elizabeth was covered in mud from head to toe. She was clearly shaken and tears were running down both cheeks.

Gently, Miss Ranger took hold of her hand.

Patrick stood, frozen, at the top of the steps, staring down at the scene in dismay.

'I'll see Elizabeth gets a hot bath and some fresh clothes,' said Miss Ranger. 'Oh, poor Elizabeth.'

'And *I* will deal with the boy,' said Mr Johns, angrily. 'Patrick Holland, stay right where you are. I am going to have a word with you.'

As Elizabeth, still shaken and upset, was led indoors by her class teacher, the senior master spoke sternly to Patrick.

'We do not tolerate this sort of behaviour at Whyteleafe.'

'I didn't push her, sir. It was an accident—'

'Yes, because your temper was completely out of control,' replied Mr Johns. 'You behaved like a ruffian.'

'I had good reason to lose my temper!' protested Patrick. 'I've just found out something. Elizabeth tried to do something extremely bad to *me* . . .'

Mr Johns cut him short.

'You will report to the head boy and girl's study in one hour's time,' he said. 'You may put your side of the story *then*. They will be very fair. But I shall be very surprised if you go unpunished, Patrick. Whatever the provocation. Until you are called, please go and wait in your common room.'

Over the next hour, as he paced up and down the first form common room, Patrick gradually began to feel calmer. His classmates had heard about the incident on the school steps. At Matron's insistence, Elizabeth herself had been sent to bed after her hot bath. Luckily she was unhurt, not even a bruise. But it was felt she should rest, have an early night. Now, as his classmates heard about the two blue biscuit tins, and how Elizabeth must have mistaken Mam'zelle's tin for the tennis tin, they began to understand why Patrick had lost his temper.

'I'm sure William and Rita will understand, too,' thought Patrick. 'I don't like telling tales but I will have to explain it all to them. They will see what Elizabeth has been putting me through. It is hateful the way she can dislike me so much!'

However, on his way to their study, he heard running footsteps behind him.

'Patrick!' puffed Kathleen, catching up with him. 'Wait! I've only just heard about it all and what you intend to say to William and Rita. But you can't. It's rubbish. Elizabeth could *not* have thought the oatmeal biscuits were the goodies for the tennis match. She could never have made that mistake. She *knew* you had made some chocolate crispy cakes.'

'How could she know?' asked Patrick. 'I kept it a secret. And besides, we are not even on speaking terms.'

'I know you're not! That's why when Cook gave her a message to give you about the cooking chocolate, she asked *me* to give you the message instead. To pretend that Cook had asked *me* to tell you. Elizabeth would never have put the slugs in the wrong tin. Either somebody from another form did it, or the trick was meant for Mam'zelle after all.'

Patrick's mouth fell open now.

'Thanks, Kathleen,' he croaked. 'Thanks for telling me this.'

He walked into the head boy and girl's study in a bemused state.

When asked to put his side of the story, he could only mumble in embarrassment.

'It was just a misunderstanding. I thought Elizabeth had done something to me . . . but she hadn't. It was wrong of me to lose my temper.'

'You must learn to control it in future, Patrick. You must learn the hard way.'

At breakfast the following morning, everyone at Elizabeth's table was very subdued. They had all heard the upsetting news. Patrick had lost his place in the tennis team. He was forbidden the honour of representing the school against Hickling Green, the most important fixture of the summer. He would have to be replaced by Roger Brown.

Patrick had moved to the farthest end of the table, away from Arabella. While he crunched his cornflakes, he stared at her, moodily.

She never once looked at him. She kept her eyes fixed on her cereal bowl, her face pink with discomfiture.

Even Elizabeth was silent.

Patrick had apologized to her this morning. He had apologized handsomely. But he had lost his place in the second team. Nothing she could say would bring that back for him. As the little girl stared at Patrick's sad, crumpled face, she could only feel sorry for him. Poor Patrick!

John Terry was released from the san that afternoon, a day sooner than expected. The doctor had looked by and pronounced him fit. Luckily, nobody else at Whyteleafe had managed to contract the infection.

It was just before tea. With joy in his heart, after being cooped up for so long, John rushed down to the school gardens. He made straight for the potting shed. He knelt down by the big cupboard and opened the door. He peered inside. He expected to find some fine specimens of lettuce in there, carefully wrapped in newspaper.

The cupboard was empty.

He hurried round to look at his lettuce patch. He stared at his plants in shock. They were almost drowning in pools of water. There were slugs crawling all over them. Most of the plants had been decimated.

'Elizabeth never came and pulled any, even though I wrote to her!' He was deeply disappointed in her. 'She must have forgotten. I'm surprised.'

Deeply anxious, he hurried to the tool shed and found a trowel and some newspaper.

Then he worked his way up and down the two rows, examining each lettuce in turn. His shoes squelched in the mud. From his fine crop, only a single lettuce in each row remained intact. One a round one, the other a cos. With nimble fingers, he gently eased them out of the soil, careful not to damage any of the fine leaves. He wrapped them in newspaper and left them in the cool cupboard in the potting shed.

'They were not the best two,' he thought, in despair. 'They were not the two I would have chosen. I only hope they are going to be good enough. I'll take them to the Church Hall tomorrow. That is the day you are allowed to leave entries.'

He arrived at tea, very late. A big cheer went up. All the children were pleased to see John fit and well again. But Elizabeth saw him shoot her a puzzled look. She feared the worst.

'Are they all ruined?' she whispered, when they found each other after tea.

'Nearly,' he said, with a brief nod. He looked hurt.

111

But as Elizabeth explained about the Special Meeting, and the dead slugs, and being banned from the school gardens, his face paled.

'Poor Elizabeth! Then . . . Oh! There's nothing else I can do. I shall have to go and explain to William and Rita.'

'But you mustn't, John,' she pleaded. 'You know it's a secret! You always wanted it to be a complete surprise. At least wait and see if you win the cup.'

'I don't expect I will,' he sighed. But he looked at her, gratefully. 'Thanks, Elizabeth. I'll find some way of putting things right for you. I promise.'

Elizabeth nodded. She had complete faith in John Terry.

Things were indeed put right for Elizabeth. It happened in the nicest possible way. John's two remaining lettuces won the cup!

At the last Meeting before half-term, he was called up on to the platform by William and Rita. John held the silver cup aloft for the whole school to see. The children clapped and cheered and drummed their feet on the floor. It was such an honour for the school. There was going to be a photograph in the local newspaper. Everybody would see what fine things they did at Whyteleafe School.

'We have another announcement to make,' said William solemnly, when the cheering had died down. 'On behalf of the Meeting, I want to make a statement. Elizabeth Allen has been seriously misjudged. When Sophie saw her with the dead slugs last week, they had come from John's slug traps. She was worried about John's project, while he was in the san. She knew his secret plan but also that it was against the rules of the competition for him to receive any help. She was simply turning the pests over with a twig, to check that they were properly dead. Stand up, please, Elizabeth.'

Elizabeth rose. With due ceremony, Rita opened the Big Book in which everything that happened at the Meetings was written down. She was holding a pen.

'The Meeting wishes to delete all record of Elizabeth's supposed wrongdoing and punishment. Please accept our apologies for our hasty judgement, Elizabeth.'

As Rita wrote in the Big Book, Elizabeth was given a round of applause.

'So *that's* what you were up to!' whispered Julian, as she sat down. There was an amused light in his eyes. 'Did John use milk in his slug traps? Is that what the jug was for?'

Elizabeth smiled guiltily.

'I didn't use any, though!' she explained, hastily. 'I'm

so glad I didn't. It would have been breaking the competition rules.'

'Our bold, bad girl break any rules?' he mocked. 'Oh, no, never!'

An instant later, they were serious again.

For William had a final announcement to make.

'On one matter, I regret to say, the Book must remain open. We still do not know who played the unkind trick on Mam'zelle. Until the culprit owns up, or the truth comes out in some other way, none of us on this platform can rest.'

Nor could Elizabeth or Julian.

CHAPTER ELEVEN

THE CORRECT CONCLUSION

THE TWO friends longed to know who had really hidden Patrick's racket in the Beast's car boot. It had been at the root of so much trouble for Elizabeth and was still not resolved. Patrick no longer knew what to think. He was so forlorn about losing his place in the school team, through his own stupid behaviour, that he tried not to think about it at all. A few in the class still wondered though.

Julian was by now deeply suspicious of Roger Brown.

Elizabeth was inclined to agree.

'I have to admit it was very clever of Arabella to realize that Mam'zelle's tin looked the same as the tennis tin and that one could be mistaken for the other. I had no idea she had so much brain power. She proved herself a better detective than us.'

'Yes,' agreed Julian. Neither of them knew that it was Molly in the kitchens who had pointed this out. 'Even if Arabella did get the wrong culprit! But you're right,

Elizabeth. I feel quite miffed not to have thought of it myself. It does provide the perfect link with the mystery of the missing tennis racket.'

'Both tricks intended to get Patrick chucked out of the second team,' nodded Elizabeth. 'The first because he would have played so badly without his proper racket. The second to get him in disgrace for playing a stupid joke on St Faith's.'

'And Roger the only chap with a motive,' added Julian.

'Well, he's *got* his place back in the team now, after all,' said Elizabeth. 'Oh, Julian,' she said, impulsively, 'I do think it's such a shame about Patrick. I don't hate him any more. He was so silly letting himself be stirred up by Arabella. She's such a mischief-maker. But I wish he could get his place back from Roger. He's the better player, anyway. I expect we'll lose against Hickling Green now!'

'You are very noble, Elizabeth,' grinned Julian. Then he sighed. 'But how can we prove that Roger's done anything wrong? How can we be sure? Wouldn't he have owned up by now, anyway? He's such a decent chap.'

They both frowned. They had been over the same ground time and time again.

* * *

THE CORRECT CONCLUSION

Soon it was the day of the big match.

Elizabeth and Julian were standing on the upstairs landing, gazing through the big window. Dinner-time was over and the tennis match against Hickling Green was due to start in exactly one hour. Last summer the match had been played away. Elizabeth remembered it was a good outing. This year it was the visitors' turn to come to Whyteleafe. The coach carrying the rival team and supporters would arrive in about forty five minutes' time.

A few Whyteleafe parents were arriving already. Some of the pupils had a half-term exeat. There had been bustle and excitement all day as children packed their cases. Most parents would remain for the big match before driving them home. Elizabeth was staying on at school over half-term for a camp in the grounds. Joan was staying on, too. It would be such fun!

Watching the early cars roll up, Julian concentrated on naming all the different makes. Elizabeth, bored by this, was still fretting about Patrick, and the mystery, and whether Roger had been to blame. She knew that Julian had been keeping a careful eye on the senior boy.

'No, nothing suspicious, I'm afraid,' he reported as Elizabeth returned to the subject, yet again. 'In fact, just the reverse. Each time I watch him, he looks more down-in-the-dumps than ever. It knocks a big hole in our theory, Elizabeth!'

She nodded. They had both noticed it. For someone who had got his place in the second team back, Roger hardly seemed overjoyed. On the day it happened, he was seen walking around school with an anxious frown. And the frown had just got deeper and deeper.

'Did you see him at dinner-time?' continued Julian. 'I thought *Patrick* looked miserable until I saw Roger's face. It just doesn't make sense.'

'And look at him now!' exclaimed Elizabeth, pointing. 'Look, Julian. There he is. I can see him. Look, over by the tennis-courts.'

The big boy had just appeared, wearing his tennis whites. Racket in hand, he had begun pacing up and down, up and down by the empty tennis-courts. He was waiting for the match. He was all ready to begin.

'But there's a whole hour to go yet!' exclaimed Julian. 'What strange behaviour!'

'Julian, why don't you go and talk to him?' asked Elizabeth, suddenly. 'I'll stay here.'

'What, accuse him, you mean?' asked Julian. For a moment his usual sangfroid deserted him. How could he, a mere first former, accuse one of the most senior boys in the school of wrongdoing, without a shred of evidence? 'Don't be silly, Elizabeth. It might just be his nerves.'

THE CORRECT CONCLUSION

'It probably is. Which means he could be grateful for someone to talk to!' exclaimed Elizabeth. 'Of *course* I didn't mean accuse him! But you never know. He might open up a bit. You might find something out. I'll keep out of the way, though, or he'll be on his guard. He knows I got into trouble over the slugs and everything. But you can do it, Julian. You know how grown up you can be!'

Julian smiled. He looked interested.

'It's worth a try,' he said.

He strolled nonchalantly over to the courts. Elizabeth watched from the window.

'Hello, Roger. Want a fruit gum?'

The big boy stopped in mid-pace, close to a wooden bench, blinking. His thoughts were far away. Someone was proffering a tube of sweets, waving it under his nose.

'Oh, hello, Julian.'

'Here, have a fruit gum. Give yourself some energy for the big match.'

'Thanks.' Roger took the sweet and popped it in his mouth.

'Gosh, Roger. You do look nervous.'

'Do I?' He sucked hard on the gum. 'Matter of fact, I am a bit.'

Julian sank down on the wooden bench.

Automatically, Roger sat down beside him. It would seem unfriendly not to. Julian was a nice kid. Very intelligent.

'Well, you can only do your best,' said Julian, comfortingly. 'That's what my mother always says.'

'I wish my father said the same! He says you've always got to play to win. You can't go through life being a loser!' Roger burst out. 'And he should know! There are so many of his old sports cups in our house it takes a week to clean the silver.'

Julian looked at Roger's big, gentle face with sudden interest.

He offered him another fruit gum. It was a black one this time, Julian's favourite, but he felt it might be a good investment.

'Is your father coming to watch you today?' he asked, casually.

'Is he *coming*?' exclaimed Roger. 'He's flying in specially. He's cutting short a business trip. All the time I've been at Whyteleafe he's been longing for me to make the school teams. I tried and tried and never succeeded, till this term. As soon as Dad heard I'd made the second tennis team, he said it was a dream come true and he'd be here to watch me play in the Hickling Green match, no matter what. He thinks I must be a late developer and he says this will just be the beginning of my sports career . . .' There was a desperate look on Roger's face, as he said this. 'As a matter of fact, Julian, I'm pretty scared of letting my father down today. It will break his heart.'

Julian, with his bright, intelligent green eyes, looked at the boy beside him, at his ungainly feet and his large red hands.

'Won't he be pleased when he hears about your academic scholarship?' he ventured.

Roger shook his head. He was deep in thought.

'He thinks sport's more important. He's too old to play sport himself now. He wants to sort of live it through me. He knows about the scholarship already. The news came through just before he left on his last trip.'

'It must have been a bit of a worry for you,' said Julian, treading very carefully, 'when you lost your place in the team for a while?'

'A worry? It was a nightmare!' exclaimed Roger, unguardedly. 'There was no way of letting Dad know. He was already in the States, you see, and there was nowhere I could telephone to stop him flying back today—'

Roger suddenly clammed up. He felt he was letting his tongue run away with him.

Julian was sitting very still. The word 'States' had sent

a little tremor through him. So Roger's father made his business trips to America, then?

Roger was lumbering to his feet.

'Well, that's enough. I can't sit here all day, eating all your fruit gums, can I, Julian?' he said awkwardly. He fished something out of his shorts pocket. 'Here – have a crisp. They're good ones. It's my last packet till Dad gets here.'

He produced an open crisp packet. Julian stared at it. The words on the front said *Southern Favorits*.

'I'm sorry, Roger!' he burst out. He truly did feel sorry for the big, gentle boy. 'I'm sorry. But I've guessed the truth. Even before you offered me a crisp!'

Julian produced the matching packet from his pocket, tattered and crumpled. He had been guarding it carefully, all this time. Just in case. 'You dropped this by Miss Best's car. The time you hid Patrick's racket in her boot. Then, when that didn't work, you tried to play another trick on him with the slugs. He thought Elizabeth had played those tricks. *That's* why he lost his temper with her and why you got your place back. But it should be Patrick playing today, shouldn't it? Not you!'

Roger sank back down on to the bench. He looked anguished.

He buried his face in his hands.

'My father's coming!' he groaned. 'He'll be here soon!

He's flown in from America specially. Please don't give me away,' he begged. 'I was honestly going to confess everything, after half-term, once this match was safely out of the way. I intend to own up at the next Meeting, I promise. But let me play today. Please.'

'I have to go and consult Elizabeth,' said Julian. He suddenly felt desperately torn. 'We'll decide this together.'

'Please let me play!' begged Roger, as Julian walked away.

Elizabeth said that there was no time to lose. They must go and find the head boy and girl and ask their advice. It was much too big a decision to make on their own.

William and Rita, without hesitation, reached the correct conclusion.

'It's all very sad,' said Rita. 'Of course Roger cannot be allowed to play. He has done such bad things but, more to the point, it would solve nothing. He would simply be storing up more misery for himself in the future.'

'His father would expect him to get into teams at his next school,' agreed William. 'The misery would just go on and on forever! Mr Brown must be made to face up to the truth. Just because he was a sporting hero himself, it does not make Roger one. His talents lie in other directions. And he must be brave and tell his father the whole truth.'

Even as they were discussing it, Roger had come to the same conclusion.

Eyes blurred, he set off up the school drive. He would wait at the gates for his father's car. He would tell him the whole truth and ask to be taken home straight away.

William was about to leave the study to find Roger when there came some alarming sounds through the window.

A blaring horn – the scream of car brakes – a cry of pain.

They all rushed outside.

A heavily built man was kneeling on the school drive beside the prone figure of a boy. He had been driving fast. He had raced all the way from London Airport, anxious not to miss any of the match.

'It's Roger!' he cried out to them in horror. 'It's my own son. I've knocked down my own son.'

They all knelt round the boy while Rita rushed off to find Matron.

'Oh, let him be all right. Please let him be all right!' Roger's father kept saying. 'What was the matter with him? He was wandering alone, in such a daze. He was right in the middle of the drive. I couldn't stop in time—'

THE CORRECT CONCLUSION

'He was very upset, sir,' Elizabeth said, quietly. 'You see, he knew another boy should be playing in the match today. Somebody much better than him. He cheated to stay in the team, but it wasn't for himself. He did it all for you.'

'For me?' asked Mr Brown. He was stroking his son's head.

'He knows you want him to be good at sport,' said Julian. 'He couldn't face losing his place in the team and letting you down.'

There was a long silence.

'I've been a fool,' said Roger's father, at last. 'Oh, please let him be all right!'

Matron arrived.

'Should we call an ambulance?' asked Mr Brown, looking fearful.

Matron kept everybody back while she examined Roger and took his pulse. Then she looked up, in very great relief.

'Pulse good and strong,' she said. 'No sign of any broken bones. I'm afraid his head must have struck the ground. He's concussed. I think he's just beginning to come round.'

Even as she spoke, Roger began to stir. He groaned once or twice and then opened his eyes and saw that it was his father who was bending over him.

'Dad, I've behaved stupidly, I've let you down. I'm so sorry—'

'Hush,' said his joyful father. He soothed his son's brow. 'I know all about it now. I'm the only one who's behaved stupidly. But I promise you, Roger, things will be very different in the future.'

There was just time for Patrick to change into whites, find his beloved tennis racket and fill the vacant place in the second team. Elizabeth had begged Mr Johns to allow him to play.

He was so happy to be back in the team. But he was sorry to hear that Roger had been knocked over by a car and had had to go to hospital for a check-up. He was very surprised to learn that Roger had been the person behind the beastly tricks, but relieved that none of it had been anything to do with Elizabeth.

So she did not dislike him, after all!

Whyteleafe defeated their old rivals that day, and Patrick put up a very fine performance. There was much cheering and clapping as he came off the court. It was his play that had made all the difference.

Patrick walked up to Elizabeth and in full view of everyone, gave her a big bear hug.

'Will you forgive me for being so beastly?' he asked, in embarrassment. 'It was so clever of you to find my

racket that day. Fancy your noticing that the boot of the Beast's car was open, just a few inches. If you hadn't noticed that, I would have lost my place in the team. Everything would have been completely different.'

Over on the bank, Arabella watched and felt grumpy. Why did people always end up liking Elizabeth?

Elizabeth just stood in the sunshine and gave a happy little sigh. She was pleased that she was staying on at Whyteleafe over half-term. It was the best school in the whole world.

She thought of all the effort she had put into trying to help John Terry. In the end, he had won the cup and surprised the whole school with no help from her at all! But she was proud to have kept his secret.

The person she had really helped was Patrick. And even that was an accident!

She still didn't know why the racket had been hidden in such an unlikely place. Though she learnt later that Roger had planned, in fact, to hide it in one of the garages – until Mr Leslie, the science master, suddenly appeared on the back drive. Roger, in a panic, had fled, thrusting Patrick's racket into the nearest car boot as he went!

But there was one thing that Elizabeth never did find out. The little song she had taught Sophie, about Patrick being made of slugs and snails and puppy dogs' tails, was the inspiration behind Roger's failed plan with the tennis tin. He had heard Sophie and her friends chanting it as they skipped one day and it had given him his brainwave.

With the Naughtiest Girl around, these unfortunate things just seemed to happen!

BONUS BLYTON

Enid Blyton has been one of the world's best-loved storytellers for over 70 years. Her interest in writing began as a child, and before she loved receiving letters from the children who read her books, she enjoyed working with them as a teacher. The Naughtiest Girl stories are inspired by real schools and experiences. Turn the page to learn more about Enid as a child and as a teacher. Afterwards, you might like to write about your school and teachers and the people in *your* class!

THE LIFE AND TIMES OF
ENID BLYTON

11 August 1897	Enid Blyton was born in East Dulwich, London. Two brothers are born after her – Hanly (b. 1899) and Carey (b. 1902)
1911	Enid enters a children's poetry competition and is praised for her writing. She's on the path to becoming a bestselling author . . .
1916	Enid begins to train as a teacher in Ipswich. By the time she is 21, she is a fully-qualified Froebel teacher, and starts work at a school in Kent.
1917	Enid's first 'grown-up' publication – three poems in *Nash's Magazine*.
June 1922	Enid's first book is published. It's called *Child Whispers*.
1926	Enid begins editing – and writes – the phenomenal *Sunny Stories for Little Folks* magazine. (She continues in this role for 26 years!)

1927	So vast is Enid's output that she has to learn to type. (But she still writes to children by hand.)
1931	Having married Hugh Pollock in 1924, the couple's first child, Gillian, is born. Imogen, their second daughter, was born in 1935.
1942	The Famous Five is launched with *Five on a Treasure Island*.
1949	The first appearance of *The Secret Seven* and of *Noddy* mark this year as special.
1953	Enid moves away from *Sunny Stories* to launch *Enid Blyton's Magazine*. She is now renowned throughout the world – she even established her own company, called Darrell Waters Limited (the surname of her second husband).
1962	Enid Blyton becomes one of the first and most important children's authors to be published in paperback. Now, she reaches even more readers than ever before.
28 November 1968	Enid dies in her sleep, in a nursing home in Hampstead.

SCHOOL RULES

Elizabeth is used to getting her own way, so it's a challenge to adapt to life at Whyteleafe where the students make their own rules. That said, the student council don't have many rules at all. Here are the ones explained to the new children in The Naughtiest Girl in the School . . .

'We place all the money we get into this box, and we draw from it two pounds a week each. The rest of the money is used to buy anything that any of you especially want – but you have to state at the weekly Meeting what you need the money for, and the Jury will decide if you may have it.'

'The second rule is that if we have any complaint at all, we must bring it to the Meeting and announce it there, so that everyone may hear it, and decide what is to be done with it. Please be sure you understand the difference between a real complaint and telling tales, because telling tales is also punished. If you are not sure of the difference, ask your monitor before you bring your complaint to the Meeting.'

In that first book in the series we learn that, 'monitors are chosen for their common sense, their loyalty to the school and its ideas, and their good character.'

Do you think Whyteleafe's rules are fair?

What rules would you establish if you had a student council?

What do you think would be poor qualities in a monitor?

Why not discuss the answers with the people in *your* class or perhaps your family?

MY HAPPIEST TIMES

During her lifetime, Enid Blyton received many hundreds of letters from the thousands of children – all over the world – who enjoyed reading her books. She took great pleasure in replying to them. She also loved meeting children and, it is said, that the suggestion for an autobiography came from a young fan who presented Enid with a list of questions. He thought he might write a book about his favourite author, called *Enid Blyton – the Story of Her Life*, but his mother suggested that Enid might write it herself. And so she did. *The Story of My Life* was published in 1952. Enid wrote about her family, where she lived, the inspiration for her books and her writing process. She also talked about her childhood. Have you ever imagined what your favourite writers were like as children – and what important events may have shaped their future lives? Here is an extract from *The Story of My Life*, which takes us back to Enid's younger days . . .

My happiest childhood times were when I was reading and dreaming, when I was playing games with other children, and when I was out in the country or by the sea. Very much like your happiest times, I expect!

The games I played were Red Indians, Burglars and Policemen, Making a House somewhere – behind a bush, or up a tree, or under a table. We had tops and hoops and marbles as the seasons came round.

We played a great many card games, because we all loved cards. So do my own girls. We played Snap and Happy Families, Old Maid and Beggar-My-Neighbour.

We also played board games such as Snakes and Ladders (and sometimes Ladders and Snakes – going up the snakes and down the ladders, instead of the other way round!). When I was six my father taught me to play draughts and a little later he taught me to play chess. That was just before I was seven. He thought that all young children should learn to play chess. I enjoyed the games immensely.

I think my father was more of a naturalist than anything else. I didn't even know what a naturalist was, at that time – all I knew was that my father loved the countryside, loved flowers and birds and wild animals, and knew more about them than anyone I had ever met. And what was more he was willing to take me with him on his expeditions, and share his love and his knowledge with me!

In those days it was considered quite ordinary to collect birds' eggs. Nowadays we teach children not to, because it distresses the birds and it might lead to many kinds gradually becoming extinct.

My father collected birds' eggs, and he had a cabinet of little drawers full of beautiful eggs, neatly arranged and labelled. One of the things I had to do to help him was to insert my hand into holes in trees to see if any nests were there, and to feel for eggs.

I never did like taking the eggs. I did so hope the bird wouldn't mind. Fortunately my father never wanted more than one egg. He never knew how scared I was of putting my hand down into those small holes. Once I heard a hissing noise down a hole, and I was sure it was an adder hiding there. I was afraid of being bitten, but I didn't like to say so.

Weekend after weekend I went out with my father. Looking back, it seems as if those days were always warm, always sunny, and that the sky was always as deeply blue as the cornflowers in my garden, or as faintly blue as the harebells on the common.

We were lucky to have woods and commons, ponds and lanes so near. We explored everywhere and everything – watching the lizards play on the sunny banks, listening to the willow-warblers singing, poking down a hole that my father said badgers had been in, looking for the white violets we knew always blossomed in a certain dell.

All my childhood was steeped in the sunshine of the woods and commons and lanes, and what I didn't find out from nature herself, I read about in books, and then searched for it again. I was perfectly happy, even when I wandered about alone, finding flowers to look up in our reference books, trying to discover what bird was singing, learning the difference between a thrush's nest and a blackbird's, and a hundred other things.

'One day I'll put all these things into a book,' I said, though I didn't tell anyone that, of course.

WHAT THEY DID AT MISS BROWN'S SCHOOL

In 1920, Enid Blyton became a governess to the four Thompson children, whose ages ranged from four to ten. The family lived in Surbiton, in Surrey, in a house called 'Southernhay'. Enid had a small room which overlooked the garden, and it was there that she wrote many of her stories. Enid's tiny class often had lessons outdoors in the summer months.

Enid was very popular with her students, because her lessons were both practical and creative. She worked with them to put on performances for which they made props, costumes and invitations – and even sold tickets.

In 1941, she published a long story called 'What They Did at Miss Brown's School', which was divided into monthly episodes. It's been hard to find for many years, but you can read extracts in these new editions of the Naughtiest Girl books. The character of Miss Brown and her tiny class is very much based on Enid Blyton and her school at the Thompsons' . . .

Here's the next extract . . .

WHAT THEY DID AT
MISS BROWN'S SCHOOL

6. June. The Surprising Silkworms.

'MISS BROWN, you've got a ladder all the way up the back of your stocking!' said Mary one morning.

'Oh dear! And these are my very best silk stockings!' sighed Miss Brown. 'How I wish I could spin pure silk like the silkworms do! Then I could make my stockings for nothing!'

The children laughed. 'Do silkworms *really* spin silk, Miss Brown?' asked John.

'John! Have you never kept silkworms and seen what they do?' said Miss Brown in surprise.

'Never,' said John. 'I've kept ordinary caterpillars, Miss Brown, but they didn't spin silk or anything exciting like that.'

None of the others had kept silkworms either. Miss Brown made up her mind at once that that should be June's fun.

'It is a little late to get silkworm eggs,' she said, 'but maybe we can still buy them. If not, we'll buy the caterpillars themselves. I'll write a letter now, straightaway, and order them. It will be June tomorrow, so there is no time to lose.'

By a piece of luck the man she wrote to still had silkworm eggs to sell. They were a shilling a hundred. Miss Brown bought a hundred. They arrived on June the second and the children looked at them with interest.

'They are round and flat, and not much bigger than a pin's head, Miss Brown,' said John.

'Won't the silkworms be tiny!' cried Susan.

'Yes, at first,' said Miss Brown, 'but later on they will be longer and fatter than your fingers, Susan!'

Susan couldn't believe it. 'What do we feed them on?' she asked.

'Well, they like mulberry leaves better than anything,' said Miss Brown. 'But they will eat lettuce too. If we could get mulberry leaves we should find the boxes pleasanter to clean out each day, for mulberry-fed silkworms leave only a dry litter behind them, but lettuce-fed ones leave a moist, unpleasant litter to clear up.'

'Well, Miss Brown, *I* know where there is a mulberry tree!' cried John. 'In my granpa's garden. I can go there each day and get fresh leaves.'

'Good, John,' said Miss Brown, pleased. 'Well, we

had better have leaves each day now, for these eggs may hatch at any time.'

'Are we all going to share them?' asked Susan, who always liked to have something of her own.

'I'll tell you what we will do,' said Miss Brown. 'These eggs will not all hatch out at once, but in batches. We will say that the first-hatched batch shall be John's, because he is to bring the leaves. The next shall be Mary's, the next Peter's and the last Susan's, because she is the youngest.'

'That will be fun!' said John. 'We'll have to have four boxes. And shall we have to cover the silkworms with glass or something, Miss Brown, to stop them crawling away. I remember my caterpillars all crawled away last year when I forgot to cover them.'

'Oh no,' said Miss Brown, 'silkworm grubs are not like ordinary caterpillars, John – they are "tame" and will not crawl away from their boxes. You see, for thousands of years they have been kept for their silk, so they have lost the ways of wild caterpillars. We don't need to cover them – but we must remember not to leave them by the open window or the birds may come in and steal them!'

The next day about twenty of the silkworm eggs hatched! The children were so pleased. They looked into the box-lid, where Miss Brown had placed the batch of eggs, and saw what looked like tiny, short bits of black cotton crawling about!

'Gracious! Are those tiny black things the silkworms?' asked Susan. 'I can hardly see them!'

'Yes – some of the eggs have hatched,' said Miss Brown. 'The grubs ate their way out of the egg-shell. Now, John, where is your first lot of mulberry leaves? Good! We will put them into this second box-lid – and then I want you to watch me lift these tiny caterpillars with my paint brush. I don't want to harm them by lifting them with my fingers, but I can easily lift them on to the fresh leaves with a brush. Each day you must do this, John, so watch carefully.'

John had placed his mulberry leaves into a second shallow box-lid. Miss Brown carefully lifted up each tiny black thread-like caterpillar to the leaves. Then she took a magnifying-glass from her desk and lent it to each child in turn so that they might see how the tiny caterpillars began to nibble the leaves.

No eggs hatched the next day, but another lot had hatched into tiny black threads the day after. Mary lifted them gently on to her leaves in a third box. There was a fourth box too – or rather box-lid – and in this John placed his caterpillars whilst he cleaned out the other box.

'We must always have an extra odd box,' said Miss Brown. 'Because we can't clean out a box while the caterpillars are in it. Now I wonder when *your* caterpillars are going to hatch, Peter!'

They hatched the very next day, and Peter was delighted. He, too, had a box-lid given him and some mulberry leaves.

Poor Susan had to wait a whole week before the last lot of eggs hatched – but as there were thirty-four she was delighted. 'I've got the most!' she said. 'I had to wait the longest, but I've got the most.'

'Good for you,' said John. 'I say, Miss Brown, aren't my silkworms growing! They are three times the size of Susan's!'

'I've got twenty-two,' said Peter, counting.

'I've got twenty-one,' said John.

'I've got twenty-three,' said Mary.

'And I've got thirty-four,' said Susan. 'That makes exactly a hundred.'

How those silkworms grew! They became a pearly-grey colour and ate all day long. The children soon found a quick way of changing them from one box to another. This is what they did.

When John came to school in the morning with his new mulberry leaves, each child put a few fresh leaves into his or her box. The caterpillars soon smelt out the new leaves and crawled on to them in delight. Then all that the children had to do when cleaning them was to lift the new leaves *and* caterpillars into the odd box and clean out the old box! They did their cleaning one by one, so there was always an odd box to move the silkworms into, and the odd box left over was clean and ready to use the next day.

One day Susan was very much upset because when she counted her caterpillars she found there were only thirty! 'Four have gone!' she said, almost in tears.

'I am afraid you must have thrown them away when you cleaned out the box,' said Miss Brown.

'I shall write down the number I have and always count them in future,' said Susan. The others did this too, for they were afraid of losing theirs like Susan.

Another really dreadful thing happened the week after. Somebody opened the window and forgot to shut it – and there, on the window-sill were the fat silkworms, eating away at the mulberry leaves.

When the children came back from their play in the garden, they heard a scurry of wings in the schoolroom – and what do you think had happened? Some sparrows had peeped in at the open window and had seen the silkworms. And they had taken at least thirty or forty!

The children were so upset. Miss Brown was sorry too.

'Well, I did warn you not to leave this window open,' she said.

'It was my fault,' said John, very red. 'I'm so very, very sorry.'

'Being sorry won't bring back our poor silkworms,' said Mary sadly.

'Well, it's a thing that any of us might have done,' said kind-hearted Peter, sorry for John. 'It's a good thing we came in when we did – we've still got plenty. And my word, aren't the silkworms enormous now!'

They certainly were – and they kept doing a most surprising thing. They split their skins, and worked their way out of them! The first time Peter saw one doing this he was quite alarmed and tought that his silkworm was ill!

'Oh no,' said Miss Brown, laughing. 'They grow so fast that their skins become too tight, so they have to split them. But it doesn't matter because they have a fine new skin underneath!'

Four times the silkworms changed their skins, and they grew so enormously that, as Miss Brown had said, they were longer and fatter than Susan's fingers.

'The silkworms always seem to feel a bit upset before they change their skins,' said John. 'But goodness, don't they eat afterwards! Miss Brown, I watched this one through the magnifying-glass when it changed its skin. It was marvellous!'

After about six weeks had gone by the silkworms

began to look a little different. The children all noticed the change.

'They seem to have gone a bit smaller,' said Mary, 'and they look rather transparent. Mine won't eat at all, Miss Brown, and look at that one shaking its head about as if it's giddy.'

'The time has come for them to change into chrysalids. We must help them,' said Miss Brown. 'Look, here is some new blotting-paper. I want you to make some cone-shaped bags like those the grocer makes for currants. Make one for each silkworm. The silkworms are about to do their most marvellous work now – they are going to spin their silk!'

Miss Brown put a few twigs into each box. She told the children to watch which silkworms climbed up them. Any that did this were to be taken up gently and popped into a cone-shaped bag.

John had three silkworms to put into the blotting-paper bags.

'Write the date on the bags,' said Miss Brown. 'Now pin the bags up on the wall in a row, John. Pin under each one a piece of paper in case the silkworm sends out a flow of water and stains the wall. There – that's right!'

Soon more and more bags were pinned up on the wall as the silkworms came to the time when they must spin. How the children loved to peep into each bag and see the silkworms spinning, spinning, spinning! To and fro they moved their heads, and the children, looking through the magnifying-glass, saw a thin thread of silk coming from their lower lips. Each silkworm had fastened itself to the bag, and was now winding the golden silk around itself.

At first the children could see each silkworm through the mist of thread – but after a while the silk was so thick that the silkworm had quite disappeared behind it. In a few days the cocoon was finished, a lovely golden case.

'Is the silkworm inside?' asked John.

'Yes – and there it changes its skin for the last time!' said Miss Brown. 'And if you could see the silkworm now it would no longer look like a caterpillar – but a chrysalis. Its skin becomes hard, like a shell, and is red-brown. It lies quite still – and a miracle happens!'

'Yes, I know what it is,' said Mary. 'The caterpillar changes to a silk-moth, with wings. I do wish I knew how it did that, Miss Brown. It's like magic.'

'Miss Brown, the silkworm I put into this bag yesterday is trying to get out,' called Susan. 'It won't spin.'

'Well, it isn't quite ready then,' said Miss Brown. 'Put it back into the box to eat a little longer. Now, John, when a week has gone by we will unwind the silk from this cocoon and you will see how strong and fine the thread is – perfect for weaving into clothes.'

The silkworms all made their golden cocoons one by one – and then, when a week or so had gone by, Miss Brown took a cocoon gently from a bag. She pulled off the loose outer silk, and found the end of the long thread that the silkworm used to spin its cocoon. Then she took a doubled-over piece of stiff paper and began to wind the silk round and round it.

The golden cocoon rolled about on the table with the pull of the silk. Miss Brown told John to go on winding off the silk till it was finished. It took him a long time! The cocoon became smaller and smaller as he wound the silk, which lay golden and fine round his paper. At last the last piece was wound – and there, on the table, was nothing but a little hard-shelled chrysalis, and the last cast-off skin of the silkworm!

The children loved winding off their silk. They had such a lot. Mary said she was going to use it for sewing!

All the silkworm chrysalids were put into a box – and then one day a surprising thing happened – from each chrysalis a cream-coloured moth came out. They had stout furry-looking bodies, and they stood about, drying their wings.

'The big ones are the mother-moths,' said Miss Brown, 'Now who would think that these pretty winged creatures could possibly grow from the tiny eggs we had at the beginning of June!'

The children took a big box and put the silk-moths into it. First they lined the box with paper, as Miss Brown told them to. They did not put on the lid as the moths could not fly. They did not even give them anything to eat, for the moths had no mouths!

'We'll leave them alone in peace in this shady corner of the classroom,' said Miss Brown. 'Then maybe they will lay their eggs for us, and next year we shall not need to buy any!'

The moths *did* lay their eggs – hundreds of them in neat batches on the lining-paper. Miss Brown took out the paper, cut out the batches of eggs, left them exposed to the air for about four days, and then put them away in a cool cupboard till the next year.

'And next spring we'll hatch out our own eggs and keep silkworms all over again!' said Susan, pleased. 'Well, that *was* interesting, Miss Brown!'